Praise

"Very engaging. Hard
Navy SEAL (Retired)

"Sweetly sentimental and moving… An endearing page-turner."
— PUBLISHERS WEEKLY

"A tapestry of emotion deeply set inside the bravest of Americans: the soldier." — MILITARY WRITERS SOCIETY of AMERICA

"Reminds me of *American Sniper* and *Lone Survivor*, but accompanied with a beautiful and epic love story that is completely unforgettable." — LAUREN HOFF, United States Air Force

"A heart-rending, white-knuckle journey into the courageous lives of our nation's heroes. Shows us the meaning of commitment—to country, and to love." — JOCELYN GREEN, Award-winning author

Other Books by Jessica James

Award-Winning Women's Fiction

LACEWOOD

Award-Winning Romantic Suspense

PRESIDENTIAL ADVANTAGE

DEADLINE (Phantom Force Tactical Book 1)

FINE LINE (Phantom Force Tactical Book 2)

FRONT LINE (Phantom Force Tactical Book 3)

PHANTOM FORCE TACTICAL SERIES SET Books 1-3

PROTECTING ASHLEY

MEANT TO BE: A Novel of Honor and Duty

Award-Winning Historical Fiction

THE LION OF THE SOUTH

SHADES OF GRAY: UNABRIDGED (LOST CHAPTERS)

SHADES OF GRAY: A Novel of the Civil War in Virginia

NOBLE CAUSE (Book 1 Heroes Through History)

ABOVE & BEYOND (Book 2 Heroes Through History)

LIBERTY & DESTINY (Book 3 Heroes Through History)

HEROES THROUGH HISTORY BOXED SET (Books 1-3)

www.jessicajamesbooks.com

JESSICA JAMES
HONOR COURAGE LOVE

Sleigh Bells

Ring

Merry Christmas, Chris!

Jessica James

"Christmas waves a magic wand over the world, and behold, everything is softer and more beautiful."

– Norman Vincent Peale

Prologue

Chad Devlin leaned one broad shoulder against the porch post of the bunkhouse as a limousine pulled through the elegant arched gateway. "Another guest just arrived for the Christmas gala," he said to no one in particular.

"Another city slicker you mean." The man standing beside him sent a slug of tobacco onto the dirt near the steps as the car drove slowly up the gravel driveway to the main house about a hundred yards away.

Chad lifted the hat off his brow and scowled at the brown smudge on the ground, but didn't say anything. Judd had been warned by Mrs. Dunaway about spitting anywhere he pleased, any number of times. It wasn't exactly the type of thing that wealthy folks wanted to see when they were *getting away from it all* on this high-priced luxury ranch in the middle-of-nowhere, Montana. And it wasn't behavior that one would expect from a man who was in charge of dozens of ranch hands.

With his eyes glued on the woman getting out of the car, Chad took a step forward, causing the coffee in his mug to slurp over the top. "Is that Jordyn Dunaway?"

Judd let out a whistle as the long-legged blonde accepted the suitcase handed to her by the driver. "I've only seen pictures." Judd leaned forward and squinted as if to lessen the distance between them. "You *know* her?"

Chad grew silent and merely shrugged, angry that he'd expressed any emotion and let down his guard. He hadn't seen Jordyn Dunaway since she'd left for a job in New York City more than a decade ago. Was that really her? Had she really come back home after all this time?

The woman paused on the porch and swept the golden tumble of hair off her shoulders, an action that flaunted a regal confidence and stately poise. Chad mumbled under his breath as another splash of hot coffee breached the top of the trembling mug, burning his hand.

Trying to slow the pace of his heart, Chad looked away and took a deep breath. Would Jordyn remember their last night together? Would she even remember *him* after traveling around the world and being away from the ranch for so long?

His gaze went back to the main house, but the door had already closed behind her.

Squeezing his temples, Chad tried to stop the memories. He even closed his eyes in a futile attempt to block the images that were branded in his mind as the best—and the worst— moments of his life.

Chapter 1

At Christmas, all roads lead home.
– Marjorie Holmes

Jordyn Dunaway opened the door to her childhood home and took a deep breath. It smelled just like she remembered…just like she'd expected—a heavenly combination of homemade cookies, buttery warm bread, and freshly cut pine from the long boughs that decorated the handrails of the grand staircase. A ten-foot tall Christmas tree, adorned with twinkling lights and embellished with brightly colored ornaments added to the charm and holiday atmosphere of the room.

Drawing closer to the towering pine, Jordyn felt a smile tug on her face at the same time a tear welled in her eye. She couldn't believe her mother had continued the tradition of trimming the tree with the same hodgepodge of holiday trinkets that Jordyn had used growing up, an eclectic assortment of baubles that seemed dissimilar, yet had one thing in common: Memories.

Instant recollections of Christmases past flicked before her eyes, vivid yet unreal, recapping some of the happiest times of her life. This serene, inviting world contrasted so completely from the one Jordyn had just left, she wondered if she'd ever have the strength to leave here again.

As Jordyn turned toward the warmth of the logs crackling in the stone fireplace, her mother came out of the kitchen wiping her hands on a lacy red apron. The silver-haired woman froze in place a moment, and then took a half step back. "Jordyn? Is it really you?"

Jordyn didn't answer until she'd dropped her bags and ran toward her mother. "Yes. I'm finally home! And it's so good to see you!"

"I've missed you so much." Her mother returned the enthusiastic embrace, and then pushed her to arm's length to study her. "You look even better in person than you do through the computer thingy. You've hardly changed."

"Really?" Jordyn laughed. "Because if I look as tired as I feel, then you're only saying that because you're my mother."

Mrs. Dunaway took her arm and led her into the kitchen. "Why don't you have a cookie and some warm milk and go straight up to bed. The next few days will be long ones, and you probably have jet lag."

"You're right about that." Jordyn nodded. "I was hoping to have a full week to help you get ready for the Gala—" She stopped in the kitchen doorway and took a long, deep breath as she absorbed the scene. "There were times I didn't think this day would ever come…that I'd ever get back to Painted Sky Ranch to stand in this room again."

She gazed lovingly around the oversized kitchen and saw that nothing had changed here. It was as if time had stopped during her long absence and allowed her to step in and pick up where she'd left off.

Racks of Christmas cookies and gingerbread men sat on the counters cooling, while a rolling pin and a large pile of dough lay idle on a wooden table to the side.

She glanced at her mother, who was already leaning over an open oven door. Anticipating her next move, Jordyn cleared a place on the table for the fresh batch of cookies. "How can I help you pull things together before Saturday? I know you've been doing this for more than thirty years, but it's still a lot of work for one person…"

Jordyn's voice trailed off noticeably as she thought about the hole left by the loss of her father. He would have been up since the crack of dawn making sure everything was perfect for the largest holiday party in the region. Jordyn's heart broke all over again at his loss.

Shawn Dunaway had always been bigger than life to her—and to everyone he met for that matter. He was the type of man everyone learned from, leaned on, listened to, and loved. With a heart as big as the Montana sky, he'd bought this failing ranch and turned it into one of the most renowned and prestigious dude ranches in Montana. People came from all over the world to stay here and be treated to an all-inclusive array of special activities and amenities.

But the ranch offered more than just top-tier luxury and extravagance. It provided a more intimate and family-oriented atmosphere than most other ranches, giving guests the impression they were extended family—not strangers. Generosity and kindness were part of Mr. Dunaway's ethos, and everyone could feel it the minute they stepped onto the property.

The impact of his benevolence was unmistakable…especially this time of year. Mr. Dunaway told everyone he created the "Painted Sky Grand Christmas Gala" to entice people to visit Montana over the winter months and holidays. But anyone who knew him understood that that justification was only partly the truth. The man loved Christmas and wanted a reason to share it with everyone he could. His joyful enthusiasm was contagious, and his love for the magic of Christmas was unforgettable.

In fact, he'd bought this sixty-thousand-acre ranch located right outside the enchanting mountain town of Noelle because of the holiday-themed name of the friendly community. With his zeal for life and his dedication to bringing joy to everyone he met, it hadn't taken long for him to become known throughout the region as Father Christmas.

The first ball had been held thirty-two years ago with about a dozen people in attendance. Two hundred and fifty guests were booked for the Gala this Saturday, and they would be joined by dozens of volunteers and a handful of local organizations. Many of the attendees would be neighbors and friends coming from nearby ranches and towns—but some were coming from as far away as Europe and even beyond.

Because of the significant impact the ranch had on the local economy, the Painted Sky Grand Christmas Gala had grown into a lavish social event for the entire town—and region—with part of the proceeds being donated to a different local charity each year.

No one really called it by the full name anymore. Now it was simply known as "the Gala." Not only did it give the local hardworking ranchers a chance to dress to the hilt and mingle with some of the most prestigious people in the world, but it brought extra money to dozens of businesses and charities.

Jordyn's thoughts drifted back to her father's funeral in February. She'd flown in for the service in town, but with multiple flight delays from halfway across the planet, she'd only had time to attend the ceremony, meet a short time with family, and get back on another plane. She'd never even made it back to the house to mourn with her mother.

"It's mostly under control." Mrs. Dunaway interrupted her thoughts. "Some ladies from town are decorating the Lodge right now, and you probably saw all the outdoor decorations when you came in."

Jordyn nodded, recalling the wreaths that hung from every window of the large log home, and the pine swaths and red ribbon wrapped around the porch railing. "I haven't seen the Painted Sky tree yet, but everything looks beautiful."

She smiled as she thought about the iconic tree, which was a unique holiday feature all by itself. People came from miles around to see the eighty-foot high spruce that stood in the center of a cluster of cabins, all of which would be decorated from top to bottom. The tree itself was one of the features that had drawn her father to this piece of property. He'd laid out the cabins and the "Lodge," a gigantic recreation building and dining hall, with the magnificent tree as the focal point.

From the very first year he owned Painted Sky, Mr. Dunaway had been the grand marshal of an official tree-lighting ceremony in November that kicked off the holiday season. The day always included a trail ride to the river, followed by a bonfire, hot chocolate, and marshmallow roasting activities.

"Oh, and I almost forgot to tell you…" Mrs. Dunaway paused as she leaned down and slid another rack of cookies into the oven. "Kristy is in the dining room decorating cookies with Lisa and Lori Connor."

The sound of laughter echoed from the room just then, causing Jordyn to walk the short distance to the doorway. "Oh my gosh. You're all really here."

The three startled women turned around from their work and stood speechless a moment. Finally, the one in the center, a petite brunette wearing a festive red sweater, shrieked. "Jordyn? Jordyn Dunaway?"

Jordyn smiled as her best friend from high school ran and gave her a big hug, followed by the twin sisters Lisa and Lori, who were a few years younger.

"Didn't Mom tell you I was coming home?"

Mrs. Dunaway stepped into the room. "I didn't want to get anyone's hopes up, honey…in case…you know…you didn't make it in time for the Gala."

Jordyn nodded. Once again, flight delays had made her three days late from her planned arrival here. She'd come close to missing the event completely, and would never have made it if she hadn't made some desperate calls to business acquaintances with private jets.

"Did you tell her—" Kristy stopped in mid-sentence, giving Jordyn the feeling her old friend had received a signal from her mother who stood behind her.

"Tell me what?" Jordyn turned around and looked at Mrs. Dunaway, who was standing with her hands innocently by her side.

"A-a-bout all the plans for the Gala, of course," Kristy brushed some cookie sprinkles off her hands as if suddenly anxious. "This is going to be the biggest and best one yet!"

"I'm not sure how it can get any bigger or better than when dad was here."

"Oh, but it is," Kristy said. "We've added so many small events during the day…and you probably don't even know that twelve more cabins have been built over by the river."

Jordyn shook her head. "I hardly recognized the stretch of road after the turn-off on the way in. But the ranch house and barns look just like the old days."

"We planned it like that." Mrs. Dunaway spoke from inside the kitchen as she moved effortlessly from stove to sink to a large old-fashioned storage cupboard. "We wanted the tradition of the main house to remain, but we had to add more rooms to accommodate all the people who want to stay. And your father envisioned those cabins for the fly fisherman since the very beginning."

"And guess what?" Kristy spoke excitedly, as if she'd just thought of something. "The forecast is for a dusting of snow over the next few days! Can it get any more perfect than that for a holiday party?"

With practiced ease, she piled some finished gingerbread men into a large jar as she talked. "Your mother said there are a few dozen people coming to the ball who have never seen snow before. Can you *imagine*?"

The statement caused Jordyn to smile. A dusting of snow would contribute perfectly to the magical party that was lovingly created year after year. Luckily, only one bad blizzard had hit them during the entire run of the event. They'd ended up losing electricity, causing it to turn into an entirely different celebration than what everyone had planned. But with her father's leadership skills and her mother's positive spirit, the guests had all agreed it was one of the most memorable nights of their lives.

"I see you guys have been busy." Jordyn swept her hand in the direction of the table that was lined with dozens and dozens of cookies—some decorated, and some still waiting for the addition of sprinkles and icing. She grabbed one and sat down. "I was planning to take a walk around the property—maybe even saddle up Blackjack for a quick ride—but I honestly don't think I have the energy. A hot shower and bed sound more like it."

"You'll have time to do all that." Her mother bent down and gave her a peck on the cheek. "I can't tell you how happy I am that you're staying for a whole week…but I wish it were longer."

"A week?" Kristy frowned. "That will fly by in no time!"

"I know it will." Jordyn stood and gave her best friend another hug. "What time will you be here in the morning? We need to catch up."

She studied her friend who didn't appear any older than the last time she'd seen her. Kristy's brunette hair was pulled back in a ponytail, accentuating her high cheekbones and the two dimples that made her look like she was always smiling. There was no sign of the stress and sorrow she'd been through at having lost her husband to cancer. It was hard to believe she was a widow at the age of twenty-nine.

"Not until about ten. I have to pick some things up in town and no one is open until nine."

"Well, I'll see you when you get here. You have to tell me everything about what's been going on at the Painted Sky since I've been gone."

"Sure thing." Kristy smiled as she said the words, but her eyes didn't reflect much enthusiasm for the job.

Chapter 2

Christmas is a season not only of rejoicing, but of reflection.
– Winston Churchill

C had Devlin lay in his cot and stared at the ceiling, listening to the muffled sounds of snoring from other ranch hands. He knew he should try to stay in bed and get every minute of rest he could. The workload today would be heavy and he probably wouldn't hit his bunk again until late tonight. With only two days until the Gala, things would only get busier from there.

But sleep wouldn't come, so he gave up on trying. Throwing his legs over the side of the small bed, he pulled on a pair of jeans and threw a heavy flannel shirt over the long-sleeved shirt he wore.

Twenty minutes later he walked out onto the porch with a mug of dark, steaming coffee and took a breath of the morning air. Other than an occasional sneeze from a horse, the ranch lay wrapped in darkness and all was quiet.

Once the sun came up the scene would change from peaceful and still to one of commotion chaos and action, with little time to rest or even take a break. There were horses to feed, cattle to move, and endless questions from guests to answer. Everyone wanted to know what it was like to be a cowboy, and no one considered the fact that taking the time to answer their questions meant the cowboys couldn't actually do their job.

Chad frowned when he thought of the term. He didn't think of himself as a cowboy. He thought of himself as a retired military medic with nowhere else to go. When his service came to a sudden halt because of an injury, he hadn't adjusted to civilian life well.

He half-snorted to himself. *Hadn't adjusted well* was the term used by VA paper-pushers. Spiraled out of control was more like it. The doctors didn't seem to understand that his injury had derailed more than his career. It had taken away his friends, his passion...his very identity. He'd started drinking heavily and hit rock bottom after hearing that Mr. Dunaway had died shortly before his discharge.

Raising the cup of coffee to his lips, Chad felt its warmth spread through him, and compared it to the sense of comfort that had come when he'd received the note from Mrs. Dunaway a few months ago. It had come out of the blue to the low-budget hotel where he was staying on the other side of town. All it said was "We still have a few things of yours in storage. Don't be a stranger."

Those few words had changed everything. How she had known he was back in town and where he was staying, Chad never discovered. But he'd stopped in to see her—on the pretense of picking up his things—and never left.

This place had always felt like home—and now even more so. The Dunaways were like the family he'd never had. If Mr. Dunaway hadn't taken him under his wing during his young rebellious years, Chad didn't know where he would be today. He'd singlehandedly turned Chad's life around, teaching him, not only ranching skills, but life skills he still carried with him today.

Chad recalled asking the wealthy ranch owner why he'd hired an unruly kid from a broken home on the poor side of town. Mr. Dunaway had merely shrugged off the question as if it were a pointless one. "It doesn't matter where you came from, son. It only matters what you're made of."

The memory of those words is what caused Chad turn the corner to his new life. There was no way he was going to mess this up and make Mrs. Dunaway regret her decision to hire him back. He'd been sober since the day he'd put his bags down in the bunkhouse, and he had no intention of ever drinking again—at least nothing stronger than Mrs. Dunaway's sweet tea.

He shifted his mug to his right hand and held out the other. It still trembled a little, but it wasn't from alcohol, and it had noticeably lessened over the past month. Every day seemed to get a little easier, and every night the muddle of nightmare-filled sleep seemed to lessen. The fresh air and hard work were good for him…inside and out.

But then his mind drifted back to what he'd seen yesterday. Was Jordyn Dunaway really home? The two of them had grown up together. They'd been inseparable as kids. But he wasn't sure how he felt about seeing her now. He made a mental note to stay as far away from the main house as possible.

Chad took another deep breath of the clean mountain air. It was unusually warm for a pre-dawn December morning, but cooler temperatures were on their way. The forecast was for snow, which would make getting the ranch ready for the Gala all that more interesting.

Leaning his shoulder into the porch post, Chad had just brought the mug back to his lips when he saw a movement in one of the paddocks.

Frustration, followed by a bit of anger, washed over him. The horses in that paddock were off-limits to the guests because they were the ranch's breeding stock and the hands' personal work horses. They were tough—and valuable—and sometimes not all that approachable. Good grief, Blackjack was even in there. He was just plain ornery and mean when he wanted to be.

The minute guests arrived at the ranch they were told which places were available for their enjoyment and the areas that were prohibited. This paddock was on the strictly prohibited list. The horses in the main barn, where visitors were *encouraged* to visit, were gentle, patient animals that were safe for urban guests who had never touched a horse before.

Chad slammed his coffee down on the porch railing and walked swiftly toward the paddock gate, trying to control his temper. It was hard to see in the dim light, but it appeared to be a woman moving ahead of him in the darkness. The lack of common sense of city people continued to amaze—and frustrate—him.

Spooking these horses could be dangerous, not only for this woman, but for the horses. Didn't she know this was a working ranch, not a petting zoo? If she wanted to touch a horse, why didn't she wait until an official function during the day? There were plenty of them, including a trail ride later this morning.

Chad was surprised the woman didn't hear him approach. He was practically stomping on the solid well-packed ground as he sought her out in the darkness. The slightest tinge of light could be seen cresting the eastern skyline, but it wasn't enough to produce any real illumination. He walked by memory alone, aided by a moon that was sometimes bright and sometimes covered by fast-moving clouds.

After moving a couple of horses out of the way by lightly touching them, Chad caught sight of the woman again. She was murmuring to one of the horses while running her fingers through his forelock.

"Ma'am, this paddock is off limits. I'm afraid you're going to have to—"

The last words melted away as his gaze landed on the brilliant green...teary...eyes of Jordyn Dunaway.

Chapter 3

What is Christmas? It is the tenderness of the past, courage for the present, and hope for the future.
– Agnes M. Pahro

The voice from out of the darkness and then the figure standing in front of Jordyn caused such a surge of surprise and emotion that she just stood and stared. It seemed like long minutes passed, but surely they were only seconds.

"Chad?" She blinked a few times, partly in an effort to her clear her cloudy eyes, and partly to see if the image remained—or was only a figment of her imagination. Her heart flailed and flopped in her chest at the sight of the man she had tried so hard to forget. The impulse to run into his arms—and run away—were both so strong, she wasn't sure what to do. "W-what are you doing here?"

"I *work* here." His voice was low and gravelly.

"You work here?" Jordyn's gaze shifted to the moon that was setting over Chad's shoulder, trying to clear her mind and slow down the tumble of thoughts running through her brain. The conversation from yesterday replayed in her mind, as did the look on Kristy's face. So this is what she had *almost* told her before being stopped by her mother. The ranch was

so big, her mother probably thought they would never run
into each other this soon.

"When? *Why?*" Her eyes went back to the man she had
once known so well, but hadn't talked to for more than a decade. He had not shaved yet this morning, giving him a rugged, cowboy kind of look. His memorable black hair curled
from beneath the brim of his tan cowboy hat, but was not
overly long. His shoulders were broader than she remembered, and he seemed a good two inches taller. But those long
dark lashes and deep blue eyes had not changed one bit. They
were still mesmerizing.

"Long story. Anyway, I thought you were a guest, and
didn't want you to get hurt with these horses." He turned and
started to walk away. "Sorry to interrupt."

Jordyn's heart flopped again, but this time it was definitely
with disappointment at his cold, detached demeanor. As often
as she'd thought about seeing him again, which was often, this
is not the way it had played out.

"Wait..."

Chad paused, but did not turn around to face her. The
fact that he seemed so anxious to get away increased Jordyn's
desperation to get him to stay. This had been her best friend
growing up...a guy she could tell anything to. Heck, people
used to think they were siblings because they were never seen
apart. Chad had come to Painted Sky Ranch to get away from
an abusive household, and Jordyn's father had somehow seen
potential in the wild, rowdy teen. From the age of thirteen to
almost twenty, Chad had pretty much been part of the family.

"Kristy said there are some new cabins that I've never

seen. Want to ride over there with me?" She lifted the bridle she held in her hand for him to see.

She watched his back stiffen. "The Gala is two days away. I have a lot of work to do."

"It's not even sunrise." She nodded toward the East where only the slightest glimmer of light had begun to show. "You're not on duty yet, are you? I don't think Mom requires you to work this early."

He turned…just his head, and gave her a sideways glance of annoyance. "Till we get saddled up and over there and back it will be—"

"No saddle. I was planning on riding bareback." Jordyn slid the bridle on Blackjack as she talked. "Saves time."

Her casual statement caused Chad to turn all the way around. "Bareback? Blackjack?" He scoffed. "When was the last time you were on a horse?"

"Phooey. It's like riding a bike."

"It's *Blackjack*," he said. "Not a bike. He hasn't been ridden in years and he was never easy to control even when he had regular exercise."

"Okay. Well, I'm going. And I'm going bareback. Maybe I'll see you later."

Jordyn watched Chad's gaze shift from her, to the horse she held, and could tell he was fighting an inner battle. It was obvious he didn't want to accompany her, but he was too much of a gentleman to let her go by herself. He'd always been protective and caring. Maybe that part of him still existed beneath the cold, stand-offish disposition he now displayed.

"Some things never change." His tone suggested impatience and aggravation, as he turned and started walking way.

"Is that your way of saying I'm still stubborn?" Jordyn spoke loudly, but tried to keep any trace of triumph from her voice.

Chad glanced back at her with a look that reflected he'd been thinking of something a little less polite than the word *stubborn*, and spoke over his shoulder. "I'll grab a bridle for Kosmo. Hold on."

Chapter 4

*Blessed is the season which engages the whole
world in a conspiracy of love.*

– Hamilton Wright Mabie

Jordyn led Blackjack around in a circle to work off his
energy. She'd had this horse since he was a foal, and he
was now…she did the math in her head—twenty-two.
But if the way he was prancing around was any indication, he
wasn't going to act his age when she settled on his back. She
hoped that her theory about riding a bike was right. Maybe
she should follow Chad's advice and grab a saddle.

"Here, I brought you a saddle."

The sound of Chad's voice right behind her caused every
hair on her neck to stand on end as she turned to see the
saddle he offered. His tone was softer now, but still carried
an edge of irritation. The fact that he'd read her mind and
anticipated her unexpected doubts about riding bareback was
unsettling.

"Thanks." She reached for the offering, but he handed her
the reins to his horse instead, sidestepped her, and lifted the
massive Western saddle over his head. "I'll do it. It's too heavy
for you and you probably don't remember how."

Jordyn just shrugged and walked to the off-side of the

black horse as the saddle settled on his back. She grabbed the cinch and leaned down to pass it under Blackjack's belly for Chad to grab, then made her way back around to watch his steady hands pull the leather through the buckles with practiced ease. Standing this close, Jordyn noticed how much Chad dwarfed her in height and breadth—and obviously strength. The disparity hit her fully as he tugged on the strap to tighten it, causing Blackjack to lay his ears flat on his head.

"Well, I couldn't do it that fast or that tight, but I think I could have done it."

Chad ignored the comment. "Let me give you a leg up. Blackjack is still too big for you."

Before Jordyn could respond, she was being launched into the saddle by strong arms, just like when she was a teenager. Memories and emotions surged through her at the feel of his powerful touch, but she didn't have time to relax and reminisce. As soon as her seat hit the leather, Blackjack began prancing right and left. Chad held firmly onto the reins until her boots were in the stirrups.

"You good? You should make him walk a little bit, so he knows he can't get away doing whatever he wants...like he used to do." His tone was not harsh, but the expression he wore was one of pained tolerance and impatience. If he felt the same tug of attraction that she did, he certainly wasn't letting on.

"Good idea." Jordyn leaned the reins against his neck to steer him in a tight circle as a way to slow him down while Chad mounted. Out of the corner of her eye, she saw him ease his weight into the saddle and settle without making a sound. His horse did not move until he gave a barely noticeable squeeze with his legs.

"Nice horse," Jordyn commented as they both turned their mounts toward the rising sun.

"Yeah. *Real* nice," he said with strained politeness. "Mrs. Dunaway is letting me use him."

Jordyn smiled to herself. Her mother thought of Chad as a son, yet after all these years, he still called her Mrs. Dunaway.

"So he's ranch stock?"

"One of your father's last purchases…" He stopped and took a deep breath. "I'm really sorry about your dad…I didn't even find out about it until after the funeral…"

"Thanks." Jordyn spoke while staring straight ahead. "I only made it back in enough time to attend the service, and had to leave again."

"So I heard."

Jordyn wondered at the coldness of the tone but chose to ignore it…until he spoke again under his breath.

"Taking pictures for a living is pretty important stuff, I guess."

The hint of sarcasm wasn't subtle—and it wasn't justified. Disappointment throbbed through Jordyn, followed by a stab of anger. She turned in her saddle to face him. "I beg your pardon?"

He shrugged, his eyes icy and unresponsive. "Nothing. Never mind."

Jordyn concentrated with all her might on breathing, on feeling her beloved horse beneath her, and on the beautiful scenery that was now cast in the soft rosy glow of dawn. Yet his words shook her more than she cared to admit. *You can't tell him anything so just let it go. Let it go. Let it go.*

But she'd been just *letting it go* for the past ten years, and it hurt. Her family, her friends, and even Chad, thought she was a big-time photographer who flew all over the world to exotic places and got paid big bucks to snap photos. What they didn't know was that the places she traveled to were mostly war zones, and that being an internationally known photographer was just a cover for her real job.

She took a deep breath and let it out slowly as a single tear rolled down her cheek. *I can't do this anymore. I can't keep up with this lie...especially not here. And especially not with him.*

No one—not even her parents—knew she'd been recruited by a government agency after only one year of community college. As far as her family and friends knew, she'd left her home at the age of nineteen to take pictures for a living.

Don't they know I would have never have left this place if it were as simple as that?

Jordyn pushed the negative thoughts from her mind, along with the images of the things she'd witnessed over the past decade. She needed this place. And she needed to enjoy every minute, every second while she was here. If things hadn't gone so badly between her and Chad that last night together, maybe things would be different now. But that was all in the past. She had to keep up the farce, even with him.

Yet already she was reminded why she'd made so few visits home. It was just too hard to live this lie. She didn't have the courage to smile and pretend it didn't hurt when people wondered aloud why she would leave her mother and father to run this place—when everyone assumed she'd stay and take over the family business.

Jordyn worked hard to suppress a gulp of grief. Saying goodbye to the man riding in silence beside her had been the hardest part of all. And now, after all this time, she had to face the fact that her feelings for him hadn't diminished. She'd pushed him and everything from her past out of her mind so she could do her job, but that didn't mean she'd forgotten him—and it didn't mean she'd gotten over him. He'd been her best friend. Her confidant. Her soulmate. When he was gone from her life, he'd left a void no one else could fill. She'd had a few relationships over the years, but nothing like she'd had with Chad. It was like living with a part of her missing.

His words replayed in her mind and stung even harder upon reflection, causing disappointment and anger to collide within her. This isn't how it was supposed to turn out. In her dreams, Jordyn had told Chad everything. And in those dreams, he'd forgiven her and understood. Fantasy and wishful thinking had made her think that someday they could go back to the way it used to be—best friends. But she was living with reality now, and the notion of any reconciliation with him dissolved in her mind like chimney smoke being whipped away by the wind.

For all I know he's married. Maybe that's why Kristy seemed so upset.

Jordyn tried to mask her inner turmoil with deceptive calmness, but Chad's unexpected appearance and unemotional attitude left her confused and reeling. Unable to think, she gave Blackjack a hard squeeze with her legs and all the rein he wanted. The horse accepted the prompt and took off at a full gallop, giving Jordyn exactly what she wanted: Crisp morning air that sucked the breath from her lungs and a speed that lashed the moisture from her eyes. She wanted to ride as far and as fast as possible...to leave the memories behind.

But instead of leaving them behind, the flash of recollections appeared before her more vivid than ever. She could see Chad holding her hand as they climbed up Bear Mountain; hear his strong laughter as they sat together in front of a roaring campfire or laid on a blanket staring at the vast canopy of stars. Knowing that special moments like those were gone forever caused a surge of fresh pain.

Her thoughts were interrupted by the thundering hooves of Chad's horse right behind her and then right beside her. Before she could figure out what was happening, Chad had moved ahead and turned his horse sideways, blocking her path. Jordyn hurriedly used the reins to turn her horse hard to the left to avoid a collision, and then slowed him down to a trot.

She was still trying to figure out what was happening when Chad rode close enough for her to see his angry—and frightened—eyes. "The ravine!" He pointed and yelled. "What are you doing?"

Jordyn hauled on the reins again to bring Blackjack to a complete stop. She could see the edge of the forty-foot drop now, lying about twenty-five yards ahead. She'd been riding straight toward it. Glancing over her shoulder, she tried to figure out how she'd covered that much distance so fast. Time had seemed to stop—or perhaps her memory of the distance was confused. She didn't think they'd ridden that far.

"What are you doing?" Chad asked again, glaring at her with cold fury. "Blackjack isn't used to running like that. He could have tripped and thrown you." She wasn't sure if he was furious or just shaken, but his next statement suggested the former. "I don't have time to be a babysitter. Why don't you go back to wherever it is you came from?"

Those words created such a surge of anguish and irritation in Jordyn that she hurled a reply without thought. "You know what? That sounds like a great idea."

She turned Blackjack back toward the ranch and dug her heels into his side. She was so angry she was shaking. Angry at Chad. Angry at the world...and mostly, angry with herself at having done something so stupid and risky.

Blackjack turned on a dime, but his next step came with a marked dipping of his head. Jordyn thought at first he'd just taken a bad step, but the next stride was worse than the first. She pulled him to a halt, just as Chad said, "Great. He's dead lame."

"I can see that." Jordyn threw her leg over the back of the saddle to dismount. "I'll walk him back, and check out the cabins later. You can go ahead. I know you don't want to be late."

"Hold on." Chad's voice was strong and authoritative. He dismounted and picked up the horse's leg, placing it between his knees, then pulled a knife out of his pocket and began to dig. "He picked up a stone is all."

"You got it out?"

"Yeah. He's still going to be sore from the bruise, but at least it won't be jabbing him on the way back."

Jordyn led him a few feet. He was still a little lame, but it wasn't as noticeable as before.

Chad remounted without another word and then held out his hand. "Hop on."

She glanced at him sitting tall and straight like a towering spruce, and swallowed her pride. "That's okay. I'll walk."

"Get on." The tone, and the way his eyes flashed a gentle but firm warning, caused Jordyn to comply.

Placing her foot in the stirrup he offered, she grasped the extended hand and was lifted unceremoniously onto the broad back of the black and white Appaloosa.

As they rode slowly back to the ranch with Blackjack in tow, Jordyn smiled as they passed different landmarks on the ranch. Every single one of them sparked a special memory—and, ironically, all of them involved Chad. Suddenly, the happiness the memories aroused was replaced with a sense of loss and sorrow. Jordyn finally just closed her eyes to blot out the images, but that only increased her awareness of his strong back moving back and forth with the gait of the horse just inches from her face.

Why is he here, God? Why can't you just let me forget him? Or better yet, why can't things be right between us?"

Despite all the time and distance that had kept them apart, Jordyn felt comfortable with him—as if they'd only been separated for a short period, not an interval of ten years. Yet conflicting emotions assaulted her now. Part of her wanted to wrap her arms around him and never let go...and another part wanted to run away and hide from the memories. She'd never met anyone who had the power to cause such turmoil—and excitement. Even after ten years, the memories were fresh and the feelings were still there.

The rising sun on her shoulders and the smell of clean Montana air were a comfort. She was *home*. Jordyn tipped her face back toward the sun, and saw Chad glance over his shoulder. "You okay back there?"

His profile was strong and rigid, the shadow of his beard confirming the ruggedly handsome appearance she'd noticed earlier. Chad had always been a strikingly attractive man as far as Jordyn was concerned, but now his chiseled features and piercing eyes held a certain sensuality she found unnerving. She almost felt like a love-stricken teen again, sitting behind a man who still caused her pulse to race and her mind to go blank. What had happened to the level-headed woman of yesterday?

She closed her eyes before answering. "Yes, I'm fine."

"I'm going to pick up the pace. Hold on if you need to."

He urged his horse into a canter before she could answer— and before Blackjack had a chance to match the stride. Jordyn wrapped one arm around him to keep from being unseated as her mount lagged behind a moment. When she felt Chad stiffen at the contact, Jordyn adjusted by grasping a handful of his shirt instead.

With the cold air filling her lungs and the sound of the two horses cantering across the open plain, Jordyn's heart nearly burst. Her father had carved out this little slice of paradise, and now it was where she could hopefully find the peace and answers she sought. But the legacy he'd left behind was more than just picturesque meadows, towering forests, and the sparkling waters of the river. He'd left her a place that was truly a home. Jordyn could hardly believe she'd ever had the strength to leave this heavenly spot.

Her calling to be a part of something bigger than herself had been stronger than the pull to her roots...But that was then.

Would she be strong enough to leave again?

Chapter 5

Christmas is, of course, the time to be home—in heart as well as body.
– Garry Moore

As soon as they got back to the barn, Jordyn slid off the side of Kosmo. "Thanks for the lift." She turned to unsaddle Blackjack and heard Chad dismounting behind her.

"Have you talked to your mother?"

Chad's voice sounded so solemn and serious, it made Jordyn turn around.

"Of course. Why?"

"I mean…about the ranch." He pulled off the flannel shirt he was wearing and draped it over the fence, revealing tan, well-muscled forearms. The rugged outdoor life of a ranch hand obviously suited him well.

"What about the ranch?" Jordyn forced herself to look away and concentrate on removing the tack from her own horse. It was so hard to be around him and keep up this pretense that they were mere acquaintances—not best friends. She had so much she wanted to tell him…things she couldn't tell anyone else, not even her mother.

"Nothing," he said, as he loosened the girth. "None of my business, I guess."

Jordyn could feel her heart start to throb more violently as she searched anxiously for the meaning behind his words. "What are you talking about?"

"If your mother didn't say anything, then I guess not." He slid the horse's bridle off and replaced it with a halter. "I'm sorry I said anything. It's not my place."

Jordyn stared at the strong set jaw and the familiar glint of determination in his eyes, and knew he would say no more if she pushed him. He was a complex man, not easy to know intimately, yet she instinctively knew how to handle his reluctance to talk.

"I went to bed almost as soon as I got here." She tried to keep the concern out of her voice. "Will you please tell me if there's something I should know?"

Looking back, Jordyn thought her mother had seemed cheerful and in good spirits during the short time she'd spent with her. Sure, she'd aged since Jordyn had last seen her, but who could blame her for being a little stressed? This was her first Christmas without her husband. That's why Jordyn had come home. She knew this holiday was going to be a hard for her mother. Truth be told, it was going to be hard on her too. But together they would get through it.

Chad looped the rope around the fence post. "Just rumors, probably." He lowered his voice. "Your dad spent a lot of time and money planning those new cabins and the spa before he died, and your mother went ahead and had them built. But with him gone, and her having to hire help to take his place...well, it's just been hard from what I hear."

Jordyn took a deep breath and stared out at the landscape. It had never occurred to her the ranch wasn't making money.

It was featured in magazine articles all over the world and had a waiting list most of the time. But when she thought about the hours her father put in to make it successful...and how much it must cost to pay someone to do that work, Chad's point seemed reasonable.

Truth be told, the ranch was nothing like it had been back in the early days when her father had first purchased it. Somehow he'd seen a diamond in the rough and promoted its rustic elegance. Over the years the property lines had expanded. The amenities had grown more opulent. And the programming was more diverse. In addition to all types of outdoor activities for guests to enjoy, they could now relax and rejuvenate at a newly built spa Jordyn hadn't even seen yet.

Painted Sky had been nurtured into a first-class luxury resort offering Western charm, awe-inspiring views, and unrivaled personal service. For five years in a row, Painted Sky was ranked as the most idyllic resort in Montana, a special place for those who wanted to reconnect with their families, relax, and be inspired and restored by the beauty of Nature.

Some cabins now came with their own firepits and hot tubs, all of them came with unmatched picturesque views. Guests could enjoy the spirit of the old West while being indulged, pampered and treated like royalty.

"Is there a foreman or something now?" Jordyn tried to sound unconcerned as she lifted the heavy saddle off Blackjack and struggled to put it on the top rail of the fence. She glanced back at Chad when he didn't answer at first and noticed the scowl on his face.

"Yes. But I'm not sure I trust him."

"Why?"

"Look. Just let me know if I can do anything to help. Okay?" He took off his hat and rapped it on his leg a few times to remove the dust, his expression tight with strain.

Jordyn studied him a moment before he started to walk away. The new creases about his mouth and eyes muted his once-youthful appearance, but gave him an air of strength and wisdom. She'd tried to convince herself over the years that they were both too young to know what love was. But now that she was with him again, she knew her heart told the truth—and it hurt now more than it ever had.

He'd already walked a few steps before Jordyn spoke again. "I'm glad you're here, Chad. It relieves my mind to know Mom has someone like you close by."

Chad came to an abrupt stop and turned, while removing his hat long enough to swipe an arm across his brow. The damp curls that clung to his forehead added to the appeal of his bronzed, wind-worn face, but his words assaulted rather than soothed. "Why? So you won't have a guilty conscience when you leave again?"

He shook his head and turned away again, as Jordyn tried to recover the breath that had been knocked from her lungs. She wasn't sure which stung more, the words, the tone—or the fact that she really couldn't blame him for keeping his distance. She'd deserted him after he'd professed his love for her. She'd hurt him.

And it wasn't hard to see that even after ten years, he wasn't over it.

Chapter 6

*Christmas gives us an opportunity to pause and re-
flect on the important things around us.*

– David Cameron

The sun was rising steadily and so was the tempera-
ture, but the dark clouds appearing to the south and
west were beginning to look a bit menacing. Tall
mountain peaks that had been touched by the sun this morning, now appeared subdued and colorless as the sky merged
with their shadowy summits.

Jordyn greeted a few guests as they made their way toward the Lodge for breakfast and took a few minutes to walk
around the magnificent pine tree. The lights were so plentiful
they weighed down the limbs, creating a photographic spec-
tacle that she knew would be shared on social media all over
the world.

That thought was followed by the realization that the last
time she'd gazed upon this wondrous symbol of the holiday
had been her last night with Chad. Staring at the tree now was
as if a chapter of her life had been closed and now re-opened,
with an unfathomable lifetime of events taking place in between. She'd been separated from her best friend for almost
as long as she'd known him. Yet the memories of the days,

hours, and minutes she'd spent with him were more vivid and alive than any that she'd spent away. Even the life and death situations she'd been a part of were more blurred and indistinct than the times on the ranch so long ago.

Is this God's way of telling me something?

She glanced up. *If it is, please spell it out for me. Why does seeing him hurt—and feel good—all at the same time?*

Staring at the tall pine brought to mind one of Jordyn's earliest memories of Christmas. Despite only being five or six years old, Jordyn could still remember holding her father's hand and watching the official arrival of Noelle's Christmas tree. She remembered the festive decorations, the excitement in the air, and the sight of the four large Belgian horses pulling the sleigh. But most of all she remembered the sleigh bells on the horses' collars jingly loudly, a magical sound that stuck with her over the years.

It wasn't until much later that she realized every activity and event at Painted Sky was deeply rooted in traditions like the one in Noelle. Her father had taken great pride in preserving and cherishing the history and culture of the area and sharing it with people from all over the world. But in addition to that, he wanted to make sure the experience was magical and wondrous—for the adults as well as the children.

A pain squeezed her heart as she thought of him, but there were no tears. Her sense of loss was too deep for those.

Jordyn turned and made her way back to the house.

"There you are," her mother said as soon as she opened the door. "I thought you were still sleeping. I made breakfast and was getting ready to wake you up."

"I went for a ride." Jordyn threw her coat onto a hook by the door. "I thought you'd be cooking breakfast at the Lodge." Painted Sky had gained much of its recognition in the early days from its homecooked meals. Her mother's reputation in the kitchen was known far and wide.

"Oh, I hired someone to cook. It's too much for me these days."

Jordyn followed her mother into the kitchen, picked a favorite mug out of the cabinet, and began to pour herself a cup of coffee. "Why didn't you tell me about Chad?" She blurted it out before taking the time to think it through.

Mrs. Dunaway turned around with a startled look on her face that made Jordyn wish she'd been a little more subtle and eased into the conversation more slowly. "Oh…you ran into Chad already?" Her mother walked over to the refrigerator, opened the door, and then seemed to forget why she was there.

"Yeah. I was *surprised* to say the least."

"Well, I was going to tell you…when the time was right. But you looked so tired. I wanted you to get a good night's sleep."

"How long's he been here?" Jordyn could tell her mother felt bad about not revealing the information, but she wished someone had warned her. It would have helped lessen the shock.

"Just about three months, honey. He needed a job, and of course, I was glad to have him. He's like a son to me." She bent down, and pretended to be looking for something in the refrigerator. "I told him he could stay here in the house, but he insisted he didn't want any special favors. It would make him look bad among the other hands, I guess."

She closed the door without getting anything out. "Did he tell you where he's been?"

"No. He didn't say much of anything to me."

That made Mrs. Dunaway stop and look at Jordyn for the first time. "He's hurting, honey. I'm not going to say anything more. He needs space and time to heal."

"From what?"

"If he wants you to know, he'll tell you. Your bacon and eggs are getting cold. Eat up. It's a big day."

Mrs. Dunaway left the room without another word, and came back with Kristy. Both of them were carrying a pile of packages.

"Oh, let me help."

Kristy laughed. "We've got them. Finish your breakfast."

"I didn't think I was hungry, but this is so-o-o good!" Jordyn heard one of the packages jingling as her mother placed it on the table. "Let me guess, you had to order more silver sleigh bells."

She nodded. "Yes, thank goodness a new shipment arrived for any latecomers. How else is Santa going to find the children who are vacationing here?

Both women laughed, knowing the story well. Jordyn had asked her father one Christmas how Santa knew where to find the little girls and boys spending the holiday at Painted Sky. From then on, every family during Christmas week was given a large silver sleigh bell upon their arrival, and was instructed to ring it loudly three times. According to the legend created by

Mr. Dunaway, these bells had special magical power that would allow Santa's elves to hear it all the way from the North Pole. Of course, each family's bell had a different sound, so the elves would know where to find them on Christmas morning.

"I've been hearing those bells ring all week from the cabins," Mrs. Dunaway said. "I think some children want to make *extra* sure Santa's elves know where they are."

"Excuse me…Mrs. Dunaway?"

All three heads turned toward the man standing in the doorway with his cowboy hat in his hand.

"Yes, Luke?"

"Sorry to interrupt, ma'am, but Judd wanted you to know we're one man short for the trail ride.

Jordyn watched her mother's shoulders droop. "Really? He told me he had plenty of men working today."

"I only know what he told me to tell you, ma'am."

"I'll fill in." Jordyn pushed away from the table. "What do you need me to do?"

"You volunteered before you even know what it entails." Kristy laughed. "You haven't changed, Jordyn."

Mrs. Dunaway walked over to a side table and started looking through papers on a clipboard. "It's a forty-minute ride to the river. Then they stop and have a snack, and come back. It looks like about two dozen people have signed up."

"Yes, ma'am. So we'll need help getting the horses saddled, and to keep the guests on the trail, answer questions, that sort of thing."

"I think I'm qualified."

Mrs. Dunaway looked both worried and relieved. "Are you

sure it's okay, honey? It would be a big help."

"Of course. I want to do whatever I can."

Luke glanced at his watch. "We're already starting to saddle up."

"I'll be there in five minutes."

"The horses all have their names on their bridles, and there's a sheet by the tackroom diagramming what stall or paddock they're in."

"Great. That should make it easy."

The man nodded his head and turned to leave. But before disappearing, he turned and spoke. "Good morning, Miss Kristy. Maybe I'll see you later."

Jordyn watched Kristy's cheeks turn red and her smile to brighten. "Good morning, Luke. I hope so."

The attraction between the two was too obvious to comment on, and Jordyn could see why. Luke looked to be in his early thirties and was built like a typical cowboy…long legs, slim waist, and broad shoulders from the hard work involved. He wore a pair of faded jeans with boots that were well-worn but clean, and appeared to have shined his large belt buckle to reflect the light in the bright kitchen.

Once he disappeared, Jordyn gulped down the rest of her milk and headed for the door. "This is going to be fun. I'm going to grab some stuff from my room and then head to the barn. Call me if you need anything."

Mrs. Dunaway was silent a moment, but she seemed to overcome her hesitation and spoke with a voice that was somewhat in control. "Honey, just so you know…Chad is leading that ride."

Chapter 7

Like snowflakes, my Christmas memories gather and dance—each beautiful, unique, and gone too soon.
– Deborah Whipp

Chad placed the bridle over the horse's head and buckled the clasp carefully before picking up his clipboard again. Other hands were busy throwing blankets and saddles onto the horses Chad had picked out for the trail ride. Most of those who had signed up were first-timers, so he needed the most amiable and calm stock on the ranch. He ran his finger down the list and mouthed the names of the horses that stood in a small paddock already saddled and bridled. "Grady. Harlo. Indigo. Jake."

"Someone go grab Dasher, Gringo, and Grump in Barn Two."

He saw a figure disappear into the barn aisle out of the corner of his eye, and then squinted at the horses tied to the hitching post outside. "Chester. Grinch. Dodi. Blitzen." He checked them off, and glanced at another sheet. A family of four and two other people had cancelled so they only needed five more.

Laying the paperwork down, he went into the tack room and pulled two saddles from their racks. As he stepped out, the horses he asked for were being led up the aisle. He was so busy concentrating on which saddle went where he didn't notice who was leading them.

A small hand pushed his fingers away when he began to feel for the cinch. "I got this one."

He took a hurried step back to keep from making contact with Jordyn Dunaway.

"What are you doing here?

"Mom said you were short on hands down here and sent me to help."

He swallowed hard, but couldn't think of anything to say. If Mrs. Dunaway had sent her, there was no way he could tell her she couldn't go. Plus, he really did need the help. A normal ride this size would have at least two more people to keep everyone moving.

But the last thing he wanted was to come into contact with Jordyn Dunaway. He'd already changed his plans for the day to make sure he didn't run into her again. The ride was the one part of his schedule that he thought he'd be safe for a few hours. Now she was going along.

"If you want to find someone else…"

Her voice brought him back to the present. "No." He gazed into her almond-shaped green eyes and then away. "There's no one else to send. They're all busy with other things. Just try to stay out of my way, okay?"

The downcast look on her face and the hint of sadness in her eyes made him regret speaking so gruffly. "I mean, I appreciate you trying to help, but I'm going to be really busy trying to keep everyone together."

"I won't make it any harder for you. I promise."

He gave her a curt nod and glanced down at his paperwork. "When you're done there, why don't you go grab Donner from the small barn for yourself? He's big and fast if necessary, but will operate on automatic for the most part."

"Sounds good."

"And while you're there, grab Vixen and Bell."

"Yessir." Jordyn went back to work just as a few of the guests began to arrive to claim their mounts. Chad matched them up with horses based on their experience and size, and directed them to wait out in the main paddock.

By the time the entire group set out, the wind was picking up in sporadic gusts. The sun was still warm when it was out, but clouds were starting to blot it out intermittently. The weather didn't seem to hurt anyone's spirits. The riders were talking and laughing and seemingly enjoying their time in the saddle, even though a few of them looked scared to death every time a horse sneezed or whinnied.

Chad had assigned Jordyn to ride along the right flank, while he took the left. A young girl from town had volunteered to lead the group. Even though she was only sixteen, she was an experienced horsewoman, and she knew the route—really the only two qualifications necessary. Being a horse lover, she didn't need anything in exchange for the work other than the horse of her choice for the ride—which the ranch was happy to provide.

"We need everyone to keep moving," Chad reminded one of the riders who stopped for a selfie. "We're on a tight schedule, but you'll be able to shoot pictures of the landscape when we get to our stop."

The young man, who wore a seemingly brand new pair of jeans, oversized cowboy hat, and a black-and-white checkered bandana tied around his neck, didn't move until the photo was taken to his liking. Then he dug his heels sharply—and need-lessly—into his horse to catch up with the group.

Chad glanced over at Jordyn. Her eyes were mere slits as she watched the man ride away. The intensity in them startled him. He could tell she was making a mental note that this was a person who needed to be watched. Maybe having her along wasn't going to be so bad after all.

His eyes clouded with visions of the past, when the ranch-er's pig-tail wearing daughter had been permitted to go on a cattle drive. Chad had assumed she'd slow them down, get tired, and want to go home. But she'd stuck it out, never complaining or shying away from difficult jobs. It was part of what had drawn him to her. Grit and grace. Beauty and vitality. A strength and stamina at odds with her seemingly delicate femininity.

Yes, at first she'd been like an annoying little sister, asking questions and being a nuisance. But later on, she'd become so much more…

Chad shook his head to clear his mind, and urged his horse into a faster gait to catch up. He was glad for the open air and the chance to go for a ride. Sometimes he found it hard to believe he got paid to do this. Although at times ranch work was hard and dirty and not-so-glamorous, days like this made it all worthwhile.

The ride went smoothly and time passed quickly as the

group arrived at a scenic overlook that afforded the riders un-
paralleled views of the sparkling, sun-dappled river. From this
vantage-point the water seemed to melt away into a calming
forest background, interrupted by stunning mountain peaks
in the distance. It was a worthy backdrop for those looking
for spectacular pictures to send home or post on social media.

Volunteers had driven in from a different direction earlier
and set up a table of snacks beside a small bonfire where
they could warm tired muscles. Before everyone dismounted,
Chad gave them his usual speech about giving their horses a
sip of water from the large barrels stationed there, and to stay
close to the fire and away from the rocks.

Then everyone slowly got off their horses, groaning when
they hit the ground. They didn't realize how hard the saddle
was on their muscles until they tried to use them.

Chad sat casually in the saddle with loose reins while point-
ing out landmarks to an older couple who were interested in
the local history. A young woman in a red hat rode up with a
large smile, making it clear her only interest was *him*.

A loud *bang* and a couple of surprised screams caused him
to reflexively grab the reins and try to regain his seat. Turning
his horse around, his gaze landed on the man in the checkered bandana, sitting on the rock outcropping with his phone
in his hand. He appeared frozen in place with his mouth still
agape. Less than two feet away lay a large rattlesnake.

Chad followed the direction of everyone's gaze to Jordyn.
She was calmly returning a pistol to a side holster under her
flannel shirt with one hand, while bringing her horse back
under control with the other. Thankfully, all but a few of the

riders had already dismounted, so no one had fallen off at the loud sound. Most of the horses were accustomed to sudden noises and hadn't even flinched—unlike most of the riders who appeared stunned and shaken.

"I'd get off those rocks if I were you." Jordyn addressed the man in a loud voice. "They can still bite even when you think they're dead."

As if on cue, the snake began to writhe and curl, sending the man straight up into the air and off the cropping.

What the heck? Chad turned his horse toward Jordyn, but the young woman in the red hat had pulled her horse right next to his, and grabbed onto his leg. "Oh, my goodness, do you *see* that?" she squealed as if a three-headed monster had just risen out of the earth—rather than a commonplace reptile relaxing in its natural habitat.

"No need to worry." Chad addressed all the riders, whose voices suddenly sounded like a beehive of excitement and fear. He wasn't sure if their anxiety was because of the snake or the gunshot, but he addressed the former and ignored the latter. "That's why I told you to stay close together and away from the rocks." His eyes burned into the man with the bandana. "The mild weather the last few days brings the rattlesnakes out to the warmth of the rocks. If you stay where you're supposed to, you don't need to worry. Now take a quick break and get ready to start back."

Out of the corner of his eye Chad watched Jordyn dismount, offer her horse some water, and check her girth. She was back in the saddle in a matter of minutes, and began chatting with a young couple who apparently wanted her to take their picture with the river in the background.

Meanwhile, the obnoxious woman in front of him had removed her hand, but still blocked his retreat. Although she was dressed in the same Western attire as the other guests, she stood out. Her cowboy boots, her hat—and her lips—were all a matching shade of red.

"Oh my gosh. I'm so-o-o afraid of snakes. Aren't you?" She looked back at the snake lying on the rock and shivered.

Chad tilted his head. "Not really. They're part of the wildlife here. Don't go where they are, and you'll be fine." This is the only thing he hated about these rides. The single women often had no interest in horses or ranch life—or even the vivid scenery. Their only goal was to hook up with a cowboy. He picked up his reins to move on, but she stopped him again. "How long have you been a cowboy? Maybe you can *show me the ropes...*"

The way she winked at him made him instantly uncomfortable.

"It's a busy time of year, miss. I hope you enjoy your stay." He tipped his hat and urged his horse forward, making a wide circle around the persistent woman.

Getting the guests remounted and re-organized for the ride back to the ranch was no easy task as short-handed as they were. But before they began their return trip, Chad took the time to ride close to the rock where the snake still lay.

Its head was shot off.

When his searching eyes landed on Jordyn, he found her sitting a short distance from the group, staring absently at the vast landscape of her ancestral home. He didn't blame her. Whether the hills were robed in the garb of spring or blanketed with a fresh coating of snow, Painted Sky Ranch was one of the most beautiful places on earth. She took a couple of deep, slow breaths, and then turned her head around as if sensing someone was watching.

"We're ready to move out," Chad said, pretending he hadn't been enthralled by the sight of her. Tendrils of blond hair that had been tightly braided when they'd started out, now whipped lightly around her face in the increasing breeze. Her cheeks were rosy and her eyes were lit with an expression of content and calm. Even after all these years, she was still the most beautiful woman he'd ever laid eyes upon.

A sharp stab of pain pulsed through his body as he relived the agony of their final night together. When Jordyn left, he'd swore he'd never forgive her. But by accepting the job in New York City, she'd forced him to make some tough decisions of his own. He'd ended up joining the military and had served with some of the most elite soldiers in the world. He certainly didn't regret the path he'd chosen. He'd loved every minute of it. Would any of that have happened if Jordyn had stayed?

Turning his horse, Chad signaled for the lead rider to get ready to move out, and took his position at the back of the group. He didn't have time to converse with Jordyn as she moved to cover the opposite flank. Even after they were on their way, both of them remained busy answering questions or taking pictures so the group could keep moving.

The constant stream of conversation and the uninterrupted pace of the ride made their return to the ranch seem to take mere minutes—not the hour that it actually took. Once they were back at the barn, things became even more hectic. Horses had to be unsaddled, groomed, and returned to their stalls or paddocks. Chad passed Jordyn a few times, but had no time to do anything other than to point her in the direction of where a certain horse belonged or where to put the saddles and bridles she removed.

He loved this part of the job too. This organized chaos is what kept him moving, kept him from thinking about anything but the task at hand. It was the quiet stretches that bothered him these days. Those were the times when his brain would go into overdrive and the memories would assault him. But thankfully, there wouldn't be too many of those here at the ranch—especially this time of year.

Chad happened to look up from the horse he was brushing just as Jordyn stepped out of the tack room with a cup of coffee in her hand.

"Sorry, boss," she said when their eyes met. "I needed a coffee break." She lifted her mug and smiled apologetically before grabbing the lead shank of one of the horses at the hitching post and beginning to walk away. She looked so perfectly at ease in her faded blue jeans and cowboy boots, holding a steaming mug in one hand and a horse in the other, that he found it hard to believe she'd ever been away.

But Chad knew that wasn't the case. He untied the horse he'd been grooming and caught up with her. "You want to explain to me why you have a weapon on you?"

Jordyn shrugged as if the question were trivial, but the tension tightening the lines of her face suggested otherwise. "I thought all outriders carried guns…for safety purposes."

That stopped Chad for a moment. She had a point there. For the most part the wildlife stayed away from humans, but it was better to be safe than sorry when riding into their habitat.

"Well, the regular ones do. But I didn't expect a *photographer* to be carrying."

He watched her face flash with emotion and knew he'd struck a nerve.

"It was good I had one, right? You were too tied up with Miss Red Hat to notice the danger." She forced a laugh. "Anyway, as I recall, I used to beat you at skeet shooting all the time."

Jordyn turned the corner at the end of the barn as if the conversation was over, but Chad caught up to her again. "Hold on a minute."

She stopped and looked up at him with an innocent smile, but the expression didn't quiet reach her eyes.

"That shot had nothing to do with skeet shooting." He placed his hand on her shoulder and spoke low so no one else would hear. "It would take hundreds of hours of practice to make *that* shot at *that* distance with *that* pistol. You want to explain this little feat to me?"

He watched the color drain from her face and sparks flash in her eyes. "Beginner's luck, I guess." She forced a laugh, wrenched herself free, and walked away without a backward glance.

Chad watched her tall, athletic figure until she disappeared, as a nagging sense of suspicion started to creep toward the surface. He didn't know much, but he knew *luck* had nothing to do with it. What was she hiding?

He'd been so angry—and hurt—when she'd left that he'd never questioned her story. But looking back now, little things over the years didn't quite add up—and they certainly weren't adding up now.

Why did weeks...and sometimes even months...pass by without her family hearing from her? He found that strange considering the close bond the entire family shared. Mrs. Dunaway had confided in him when he'd arrived at the ranch a few months earlier that she never really knew where Jordyn was—only where she'd supposedly been.

His mind drifted farther back, to the last time he'd seen her. They'd gone on a late-night ride, with the moon so bright on freshly fallen snow it had seemed almost like day. He remembered her laughter and her beautiful eyes, and thinking to himself that he wanted to spend the rest of his life with her.

He hadn't had the nerve to tell her during the ride, but once they'd returned and stood gazing at the huge Christmas tree, he'd finally let his feelings be known. With the bright lights of the tree on her face, he'd told her he loved her—and he'd kissed her for the first—and the last—time.

Chad swiped his hand over his eyes to stop the memory, but it did no good. She'd told him she would never love anyone like she loved him—and then she'd informed him that she'd been offered a job in New York City that she felt she had to take.

The memory of what happened after that remained a blur... probably because deep down inside, Chad never believed she would leave her family and the ranch. She was close to both her parents and loved this place with every fiber of her being.

Yet she'd packed up and left.

Chad watched a family walk by smiling and laughing as they discussed the fun they'd had on the trail ride. Their joy and enthusiasm only caused the pain in his heart to increase. Memories were being made, just like Mr. Dunaway wanted. But his own memories of this place were suddenly more painful than enjoyable. He knew Mr. Dunaway would hate that so he forced them from his mind.

Still, he recalled what Jordyn had told him before she'd left, insisting she hadn't accepted the job for the money, or the prestige, or the chance to travel.

What else was there? And why hadn't he pressed her on it?

He didn't have time to ponder the question long. Loud shouts from outside the barn sent him running.

Chapter 8

*Seeing is believing, but sometimes the most real things
in the world are the things we can't see.*

– The Polar Express

It took only a second for Chad to see the chaos and con-
fusion was taking place in a corral right outside the barn.
By the time he was close enough to get a better look,
he could see Jordyn was down on her knees working over
the prone figure of one of the younger ranch hands. She had
already removed her bandana and was tying it around the
young man's arm.

"What's your name?" Even from this distance, Chad could
hear her voice. It sounded calm despite the messy scene.

"Adam," the young man answered.

Jordyn glanced up just then and noticed his approach. "Do
you have your medic bag?" she asked. "He's losing a lot of
blood."

Chad took off for his truck and returned with his kit in less
than a minute. "Is it an artery?"

She shook her head. "Looks like he hit the fence when he
fell. Sliced his arm open pretty deep. There's a lot of blood,
but it's not spurting."

"Keep pressure on it." Chad pulled a package out of his

bag and ripped it open, then maneuvered the special bandage around Jordyn's red-soaked fingers.

"I had one of the guests go get Kristy from the house," she said. "She knows more about this stuff than I do."

"Good." Chad nodded. "I know she's an RN, but you're doing fine. Put some pressure up here."

Jordyn did as she was told, and then continued to talk to Adam. "You hanging in there?"

He nodded, though his eyes were closed. "Doesn't hurt much, but I don't like seeing all that blood."

Within moments, Kristy arrived and knelt down beside her. "Luke's getting his truck. We can put him in the back seat and drive to the hospital. It will be faster than calling an ambulance."

Chad continued working as they talked, splinting the arm to keep it immobile and prevent the bleeding from getting any worse.

"You okay to get into the truck?" he asked Adam as Luke backed his truck up to the scene.

"Yeah, I'm good."

Though shaken, Adam was able to stand with some assistance from Chad, and to climb into the seat.

After they pulled away, Chad began cleaning up the debris he'd left as Jordyn tried to calm the nerves of what bystanders remained. When everyone finally meandered away to their next activity, he turned to her. "Did you see what happened?"

"Some of it...out of the corner of my eye." She looked around as if still a little dazed. "Someone threw something at his horse. It bucked, and he flew off, hitting the fence."

Chad stopped. "*Threw* something at a horse? Who would do that?"

There was no pause. "The guy in the checkered bandana."

Both of them gazed around, but there was no sign of the man now.

"I saw him talking to that guy over there, earlier." Jordyn pointed to a man standing in the doorway of the barn. "You know him?"

Chad's gaze focused on Judd, and a tinge of suspicion began inching its way up his spine.

"Yeah. I know him."

"I've never met the man, but he doesn't look very friendly or sociable. I'm not sure he's the kind of person we should have working here. I'm going to talk to Mom about him."

"Well, we've been short-handed—and with the Gala, she probably isn't going to want to increase the workload on everyone else."

"Really? Because I haven't seen him doing much."

"Me neither. But he's the boss, so..."

"Wait." Jordyn looked up at him. "*He's* the foreman Mom hired?"

Chad hit his hat against his leg a few times before answering. "Yeah. I don't know if you heard, but old Charlie died kind of suddenly. This guy apparently showed up at the right time with acceptable credentials. I guess Mrs. Dunaway was a little overwhelmed at the time—with your father just passing—and hired him on the spot."

Jordyn stood with her hands on her hips gazing in the direction of the bunkhouse. "If I have any say, he'll be *fired* on the spot."

"It's not that easy to do in Montana." He paused and let out his breath. "Plus, I heard there's a contract."

Jordyn jerked around. "What?"

Chad pushed his hat up off his forehead. "Might be hearsay, but that's what I heard."

"Why would Mom do that? Everything around here has always been done with a handshake."

"Maybe because the ranch work was something your dad always took care of. And since she had no one else to help her, she felt pressured into making a decision."

Chad wasn't sure whether it was his words or the way he said them that caused the angry reaction from Jordyn. She took a step toward him and jabbed her finger at his chest. "You don't have to sound so *accusatory!*"

He held his hands up innocently. "Based on your reaction, I'd say you might have a guilty conscience."

Jordyn didn't respond other than with a look of grief and pain. Then she turned and started to walk away. "Thanks for your help."

"No. Wait." Chad felt instantly sorry for the look of torment that had crossed her face. "I'm sorry." She stopped walking but didn't turn around so he spoke to her back. "To tell you the truth I feel guilty about it too. I got here after Judd was hired. I should have stopped by and checked on your mom sooner."

He kicked the dirt with the toe of his boot as he thought about the months he had wasted in a drunken stupor rather than helping out at the ranch.

Jordyn glanced back at him as if to see if his words were sincere. She appeared to accept his apology, though she didn't say so. "What's going on with the sudden shortage of hands anyway? Painted Sky has always had a waiting list of people wanting to work here."

"According to Luke, it all started when Judd was hired as the foreman. Men started quitting. Things started happening."

"Like what kind of things?" She turned and faced him now, her anger apparently forgotten.

"I don't know. You can just tell things aren't like they used to be. At first, I blamed it on your dad not being here, but things aren't adding up."

Jordyn nodded and stared over his shoulder. "I'll get to the bottom of it."

"Really?" Chad couldn't help himself. "You show up after ten years of gallivanting around the world, and think you're going to fix everything here in a week?"

Her gaze darted back to his and her brow furrowed. "It wasn't my choice to be away, Chad. I told you—"

"Right. I remember." He bounced his palm off his forehead. "It wasn't your choice. How could I forget?"

Chad knew he was being harsh, but he couldn't help it. She'd hurt him, and he was just now realizing how deep the pain went. The fact that he could still feel this much emotion after more than ten years made him angry. Why couldn't he just forget about her? Move on?

Still, he knew that lashing out like this wasn't fair to her—and it certainly wasn't making him feel any better about himself. As he threw the strap of his medical kit over his shoulder, he tried to sound conciliatory. "You should probably go change clothes."

Jordyn looked down as if seeing her blood-soaked hands and shirt for the first time, and nodded absently. "Yeah. Let me know if you need any help in the barn."

Chad watched her walk back toward the house and felt a wave of empathy for her. Yes, she'd been traveling the world for the past decade doing who knows what, but she'd come home for the holidays only to find a tangle of unexpected problems. He needed to put the past behind him, and try to support her and Mrs. Dunaway. He let out a long sigh.

No matter how hard that was going to be.

Chapter 9

*At Christmas, play and make good cheer, for
Christmas comes but once a year.*

– Thomas Tusser

As Jordyn made her way back to the house, she noticed a number of young children laughing and holding something small in their hands. Their faces were lit with pure joy as they ran around searching high and low for more hidden objects.

Before Jordyn could grab the memory that was slowly surfacing, a couple walking by her pointed to the same children. "Oh, look. Someone found a *Believe Bell*," one of them said.

Jordyn nodded as it all started coming back. Her father loved creating special, magical moments that couldn't be found anywhere else—especially for children. With the world outside Painted Sky Ranch progressing and technology advancing, he wanted a simpler, more traditional, old-fashioned experience they would remember forever.

The idea for the *Believe Bells* came about when Jordyn found a sleigh bell lying in front of the house one Christmas Eve. Instead of explaining to her that it had probably come from one of the horse's collars, her father told her it must have fallen off Santa's sleigh. Every year after that, Jordyn would search for fallen sleigh bells—and every year she would find one.

It amazed her that they were never the same. Sometimes a slightly different color. Other times a distinctive shape. Always with their own unique sound. As she grew older, Jordyn had her suspicions about where they were coming from, but it wasn't until she was getting ready to leave for New York that her father confessed the truth about what he'd done so that his baby girl would keep "believing."

Jordyn stopped in mid-step as it occurred to her that she didn't have anything tangible to hold from those days. Every year on Christmas Eve, her father would tell her to place the bell on the front porch so Santa could put it back on the sleigh. Jordyn smiled to herself as she remembered running onto the porch every Christmas morning before she even looked under the tree. It filled her heart with joy to discover that Santa had taken the bell.

The thought of his simple act of love caused Jordyn's eyes to well up with tears. Her father had been larger than life when he was alive. And even after he was gone, his spirit continued to live on in the traditions and love that still flowed through Painted Sky Ranch.

She could see it on the faces of the children as they searched for their own sleigh bells, because of course, the practice had eventually grown to include everyone at the ranch. Her father had woven an elaborate story about a select group of elves—the Sleigh Bell Elves—who would come hide bells all over the ranch. Upon their arrival, each family received their own special jar to decorate and collect the bells they found.

A tag on the jar said: *With every bell that you receive, Santa knows that you believe.*

Guests could either take these treasures home with them at the end of their trip, or put them out on the porch of their cabin for Santa to pick up. If they left the jar for Santa, they would find a note in the morning that said: *Thank you for the Sleigh Bells. Their jingling sound will remind Santa of your family's kindness as he delivers presents all over the world.*

Jordyn remembered the delight her father would take out of watching even the most skeptical adult's face light up when they stumbled across one of the bells. As the jars began to fill, the excitement for Christmas day intensified. People came to Painted Sky now as much for the tradition and the anticipation of the *Believe Bells* as for the scenery and relaxation.

Of course, that wasn't the only special treat. Each cabin came with its own small Christmas tree and a box of ornaments to decorate it. There were classic movies and books, as well as plenty of hot chocolate and popcorn too. Special requests were often fulfilled by volunteers dressed as elves.

Jordyn thought about her last Christmas at Painted Sky. She'd been a young woman by then, but she'd found a bell and put it on the porch as was her custom. And just like every other time, it had been gone Christmas morning, though Jordyn had only looked as an afterthought. She'd spent most of the night in tears after telling Chad that she'd be leaving for New York.

She wondered briefly what had ever become of all those bells. Had her dad kept them? Or had he used them on any of the dozens of harnesses he'd collected over the years? She'd have to remember to ask her mother.

Of all the Christmas traditions started by her father, this one was perhaps the most memorable. No matter where Jordyn was in the world on Christmas Eve, she always took time to close her eyes and remember the magic she felt finding that special gift and giving it back to Santa.

Chapter 10

The joy of brightening other lives becomes for us the magic of the holidays.

– W.C. Jones

"Is everything all right out there?" Mrs. Dunaway wore a bright red dress with a black belt and had her silver hair swept back in a loose bun. For the first time, Jordyn noticed how much smaller her mother was compared to the last time she'd seen her. She'd never been heavy, but had a plump face that was always smiling. She looked downright slender now.

"There was an accident, but nothing to worry about." Jordyn watched her mother's face turn to worry. "Adam, one of the younger ranch hands was injured. He's on the way to the hospital. Kristy went along."

"How bad was it?" Her mother's gaze swept Jordyn's hands and clothes. "Oh, dear."

"It's not as bad as it looks. I'm going to go get cleaned up. Then I'm ready for my next assignment."

"Well, you have three more hours until the opening cocktail party tonight at the Lodge. It will be non-stop until Christmas after that."

As Jordyn headed to her room, she passed a large mirror

on the landing at the top of the stairs. She couldn't believe how bad she looked. No makeup. Hair a mess. Face streaked with dirt and blood. She hurried to her room to clean up.

After taking a hot shower, Jordyn tried on a few of the outfits that she'd sent to the ranch ahead of time. She selected a simple red dress with a black pattern that looked festive and comfortable enough for the evening events. With her hair blow dried and twisted into a simple bun, she went back down the stairs to see how she could help.

The house was alive with activity now, but her mother was nowhere to be found. Guests stood talking and laughing in front of the huge fireplace while volunteers and staff scurried to keep everything running on time.

Jordyn made her way through the kitchen pantry to the little room her mother used as an office, and found her sitting at the desk staring at a piece of paper in her hand with a blank look on her face.

"How are things going?" Jordyn asked in a cheerful voice from the doorway.

Her mother jumped and put the paper down quickly before turning around with a forced smile. "Everything's going fine, honey. You look beautiful."

"A little bit better than I did an hour ago anyway." Jordyn smiled as she continued into the room. "I heard…umm… that you're short on ranch hands."

Her mother's head tilted and her eyes narrowed. "Who told you that?"

Jordyn shrugged, not wanting to get Chad in trouble. "I

just overheard, that's all."

"I don't want you worrying about things like that. You're here to relax."

"I'm here to help." Jordyn took a deep breath and let it out slowly. "And if I'm needed, I'll stay."

Again, Mrs. Dunaway seemed to jolt with surprise. "*Stay?* You mean for longer than a week?"

"I mean, stay...as in stay. I'm at the end of my contract and I haven't extended it...yet."

"But you plan to extend it, right?"

Jordyn's mind spun as she tried to come up with a feasible answer. She'd spent ten years in service to her country. Was that enough? Was there a new chapter waiting for her here now? If she stayed, would it cause Chad to leave? Would he be stubborn and inflexible...run away from the memories? It was like a dream come true to have found that he was back at the ranch, and yet they were still as distant as two people could be. If only they could pick up where they'd left off...go back to the way it used to be.

But some things just weren't meant to be, she reasoned with herself. Even good 'ol St. Nick himself would have a hard time fulfilling *that* Christmas wish.

"I don't know." Jordyn sat down in a chair beside the desk. "I came here to think about it and pray. I'm hoping to get some guidance."

Mrs. Dunaway leaned forward and squeezed her arm. "Honey, I'd love to have you stay...but I don't want you to feel obligated. I'm doing fine."

"Are you sure?" Jordyn leaned forward to look her mother

in the eyes. "I want to be where I'm supposed to be…wherever that is. I know it's hard for everyone to understand, but I've been following a calling the last ten years. It was what I was supposed to be doing…"

"But now?"

Jordyn shifted her gaze to the framed picture of her father on the far wall. "Now, I feel like I'm supposed to be doing something else." She stared hard at the enlarged photograph, and could almost hear her dad's bellowing laughter coming from the wall. Jordyn couldn't remember ever seeing him sad or in a bad mood. He was like a force of nature, with an enthusiasm and passion for life that was unmatched by anyone else she'd ever met.

She exhaled loudly. "I'm really confused, Mom."

"Well, you've come to the right place to figure it out. I'm really glad you're here."

Jordyn noticed that her mother casually pulled some other papers over the one she'd been reading as she talked.

"What were you looking at just now?"

"Oh, nothing." Mrs. Dunaway put her hand flat down on the stack of papers. "Just some boring business correspondence."

"Mind if I take a look?"

Her mother stiffened and sat awkwardly still as an uncomfortable silence fell upon the room.

"It's just a letter that I got…"

"About?"

Mrs. Dunaway swallowed hard. "It's really nothing."

"You know I'm not leaving until I see it." Jordyn crossed

her arms.

A slight smile flickered on her mother's lips. "Stubborn. Just like your father." Slowly she moved her hand from the top of the desk, allowing Jordyn to slide the piece of paper from the stack.

After reading just the first sentence, Jordyn stopped and lifted her eyes. "You're not considering this, right?" The paper in her hand began to shake.

"I-I'm not sure. Keeping this place together is a lot of work, honey. And I'm not as young as I used to be."

"But it was dad's *dream*." She stared at her mother, stunned that she hadn't just thrown the piece of paper into the trash. "It's become everything he wanted and more."

"The truth is, we have good years and bad years," Mrs. Dunaway said, her voice growing a little louder. "What they are willing to pay to buy it would—"

"But you *can't!*"

Her mother stood and grabbed the document out of her hand. "You don't have any right to tell me what I can't do when you haven't been here for the past ten years to help. This place is a lot of hard work. I'm tired."

Jordyn's anger and dismay were instantly replaced by regret. "You're right. I'm sorry." She stood and drew her mother up into her arms. "I've been so wrapped up in my own problems that I've been blind to what's going on here."

"No, honey. I'm sorry I let you see it." Her mother took a deep breath as her composure returned. "I don't want you to worry about such things. You're here to enjoy the holiday."

Jordyn took a step back and squeezed her temples to help

her think. She was accustomed to making split-second decisions and handling unpredictable problems, but this one hit her in the gut.

"Can you just put it aside for a while until things settle down here? I mean, it's Christmas for goodness sake, the busiest time of the year. I'm sure you're at your wit's end with preparing for the Gala."

Mrs. Dunaway shook her head. "I'd love to." She picked up the paper and pointed. "The offer only stands until December 26."

Jordyn took a step back and lowered herself into the chair behind her.

"Since you want to know what's going on, I'll be straight with you, Jordyn." Her mother pulled a folder out of a drawer. "Those cabins by the river really set me back. The cost was almost double the estimate I was given by the foreman. It's going to take a few years to break even. And that's if nothing else goes wrong."

"What do you mean by *nothing else?*"

"You know, things happen…" She stared at the wall absently. "Seems like a lot of things lately, all at once. We've had problems with the hired help lately, and matters that I think are being taken care of, aren't. It's just too much for one person to do."

"How can we be short-handed and have trouble with hired help?" Jordyn asked. "People love working here. Some of them say they love it so much, they'd work for free."

"I don't know." Mrs. Dunaway brushed away a tendril of hair that had escaped from her bun. "Judd keeps telling me we have a full roster, and then says we're short-handed. I have no idea what's going on, and I just don't have time to deal with the barn work when I'm busy with the house and the guests. Now that Chad's here, it's gotten a little easier, but..." Her gaze fell to her hands that were clenched in her lap. "I miss your father so much."

The conversation with Chad about the man named Judd crept back into Jordyn's mind, which suddenly came alive with a torrent of racing thoughts. "Those cabins by the river that you said cost more than the estimate. Who gave you the estimate?"

"Judd, the foreman, of course. I mean that's why I hired him, to take care of details like that. What do I know about building cabins?" She shook her head. "If only Chad had come back earlier, I know things would have been different. I can trust him with anything."

Jordyn leaned forward and looked her mother straight in the eyes. "Why don't you fire the foreman and give the position to Chad? Or let me do it if you don't want to be part of any dispute."

Mrs. Dunaway took a gasping breath that sounded almost like a sob. "Because I signed an agreement with him...I didn't think it was any big deal at the time, but that coupled with Montana's law makes it really hard."

"Give it to me." Jordyn only grew more determined. "I'll give it to a lawyer and find out how to get out of it."

"Don't you think I've already done that?" Mrs. Dunaway put her face in her hands. "I'm such a fool. Your father would be so disappointed in me."

"No, he wouldn't. Because you're not a fool." Jordyn pulled her mother to her feet again and threw her arms around her. "Here's what we're going to do." Her voice carried a tone of confidence and conviction that she didn't really feel, but her mother seemed to gain comfort from it. She looked up at Jordyn with big, hopeful eyes.

"Number one, you're not going to worry or think about this for another minute. I'm home now and I'll take care of it." Jordyn didn't wait for her mother to respond. "And number two, you're going to go out there and have fun and enjoy the holiday like Dad always did. Deal?"

"But how—"

"I'm going to shoulder some responsibility, and take care of it. You have to promise we have a deal."

Her mother's tired eyes looked only slightly reassured, but she nodded her head enthusiastically enough. "Deal."

Chapter 11

Remember this December, that loves weighs more than gold.
– Josephine Daskam Bacon

They were just turning to leave the room when Chad appeared, knocking twice on the wooden doorjamb to announce his presence.

"Sorry to interrupt."

"That's all right. We were just heading to the kitchen." Jordyn could tell by the look in his face that he wasn't there to socialize. "What's up?"

"One of the horses from the ride this morning is colicky. I could use some help…"

Jordyn started walking out of the room before he'd even finished his sentence. She grabbed an old coat and a pair of rubber barn boots as they passed by the mudroom and hopped across the floor as she pulled the over-sized boots on without stopping.

"That's what you're wearing to the barn?" Chad looked her up and down incredulously. She wasn't sure if he was referring to her dress or the fact that she'd just put boots on overtop three-inch heels. "And this." She stuck her arms through a knee-length coat and buttoned it up to protect her dress, but tottered a bit in the uncomfortable and unnatural combination of heels and boots. "Let's go."

When Chad opened the door for her and stood to the side to let her pass, she noticed the bandage on his hand.

"You're hurt. What happened?" She took his hand and examined the bandage that was thick with gauze but still showed signs of blood seeping through.

He jerked it away before she could get a good look and closed the door behind them. "Just a little cut. It's fine."

The sting of the cold winter air hit Jordyn as soon as she exited the house, jolting her thoughts away from Chad. Temperatures had dropped considerably since their ride this morning, making her thankful for the beautiful weather they'd had. She pulled the coat more tightly around her. This was more like the Montana winters she remembered, when snow would blanket the landscape, turning the expansive terrain into a pristine vista of snowcapped peaks and vast plains of white. Guests who witnessed the winter wonderland at the ranch would never forget it.

Chad nodded toward the small barn to her right and they walked in silence down a stone pathway. She only had to reach out for the support of his strong arm once when her left heel went a little sideways, but she quickly righted herself and then withdrew her grasp. She didn't see Chad's reaction, but she had no doubt he'd rolled his eyes at the choice of her footwear.

Stepping ahead of her when they arrived, Chad slid the door open for them to enter. Jordyn saw him wince at the pain the action caused but she didn't bother to comment on it. He wouldn't tell her anything about his injury, so why should she bother?

"It's Bell. She's in the last stall on the right," he said, while closing the door.

Jordyn paused and looked back. "I remember her. She's the pretty bay mare."

When she entered the stall, Jordyn saw that the horse was sweaty and stomping her feet to show her discomfort. "Hey, girl. Not feeling good so close to Christmas?" She lifted Bell's lip and pressed a finger against her gums, then bent down and checked her pulse near her hoof.

When she straightened back up, Chad was handing her a stethoscope through the open door. "What do you think?"

Jordyn stared at the stethoscope as a whirlwind of images swirled through her mind. This stethoscope had belonged to her father. The large silver disc made it unmistakable. A long time ago, when she was just a freckle-faced kid, he'd taught her everything he'd known about treating horses. And when she was a young teen, she'd thought she wanted to be a veterinarian and had spent the summer going on calls with the local vet.

Taking the instrument, she moved to the horse's left side and listened for any signs of rumblings from her digestive tract. Then she moved to the other side and did the same thing. "Not hearing much here."

"I didn't either," Chad said. "I was going to go ahead and start an IV, but..." He held up his bandaged hand. "It's a little awkward."

"You going to tell me what you did?"

He shook his head. "It was stupid. One of the horses got

loose and I grabbed the rope as he ran by. It had a metal piece on the end of it that sliced my finger open. No big deal."

"How'd the horse get loose?"

"I don't know the answer to that one. I tied him up my-self."

"Any chance the guy with the checkered bandana was hanging around?"

Chad looked at her as if the thought hadn't occurred to him. "I'm not sure. I didn't see him if he was."

Jordyn turned her attention back to the horse. "Well, it's been a while, but I guess I can still do this. Starting an IV on a horse is a lot easier than doing one on a human."

Chad didn't hesitate a beat, as if he'd been waiting for just such an opening. "And you've had experience with both?"

Jordyn almost fell into the trap but stopped herself before she nodded. Instead she looked back at Chad with a confused look on her face that was only partially feigned. "I don't know what you mean."

"I mean, I guess it's just another skill you picked up as a photographer," he said, with his head tilted to the side skep-tically. "It kind of goes along with knowing how to stay calm and stop the blood flow when someone slices their arm wide open on a fence post."

Jordyn turned away so he couldn't see her face and slid her hand over the horse's back. "You called the vet already, right?" She tried to change the subject, hoping he wouldn't press her on the topic anymore. She wasn't sure she could find it within herself to lie to him. "We can start fluids as a precaution, but she needs to be examined."

"You didn't answer my question."

"You didn't answer mine either." Jordyn continued to pretend she was busy checking the horse so she could avoid Chad's eyes. He knew her better than anyone else in the world. He'd catch any hesitation, any sign, or any trace of anxiety. Heck, he could probably already see how strongly her heart was beating in her chest, and sense her discomfort. "Is the vet on his way?"

"I asked mine first." He spoke in a firm, unwavering tone as he handed her a pair of sealed gloves. Jordyn didn't need to look at his face to know that it reflected the determination and resolve of someone accustomed to being in charge...of being respected and deferred to. It made her doubt her own ability to continue to keep up the charade that she wasn't still in love with him.

As she opened the gloves and slid them on, Jordyn could feel a flush of heat rising to her face, and wished she had removed the coat before starting the procedure. She tried to appear unflustered as Chad handed her some alcohol swabs and then the catheter, but she could feel his eyes on her, making her shaky and insecure.

Holding the vein off with one hand, she slid the needle into the mare's neck so smoothly the horse never moved. She watched the tubing turn red before attaching the bag of fluids Chad had hung in the stall and then opened the valve and made sure everything was flowing properly.

"I asked mine first," he said again as he calmly handed her a roll of tape. Then he leaned his shoulder into the doorway and crossed his arms, making it clear he intended to hear an answer.

Jordyn wrapped the horse's neck to keep the catheter in place, stalling for time as she tried to come up with a reasonable answer. "Look, this horse is sick. I don't really have time to bicker with you about this right now."

"I'm not bickering. I just asked a question."

Jordyn met his gaze for the first time and stared for a few long seconds into his blue eyes. His implacable expression was unnerving, but she willed herself to be strong.

"Don't ask me things I can't talk about. Okay?" She pulled the gloves off with a loud snap that she hoped signified the end of the conversation.

"Things you can't talk about…let's see, there's a list isn't there?" He pretended to pull a tablet of his pocket and held it in front of his eyes. "Being able to shoot a head off a rattlesnake from horseback at twenty yards? There's one for you. And we can add being able to start an IV after supposedly not touching one for more than ten years. That's pretty amazing, Jordyn. What other skills do you have that no one knows about?"

His tone was full of anger…disappointment…pain—and it caused Jordyn's heart to splinter and break. Why did he have to make this even harder than it already was?

She sidestepped him and headed toward the door—a tremendous effort on her part as she fought the impulse to throw herself into his arms and tell him everything. But what would be the use? Yes she regretted leaving him, and would do anything to change certain decisions. But it was over. Done. There was nothing she could do about it now. Ten long years stood between them. A full decade of not seeing each other—or even conversing. And the heartache of separation hadn't ended because they were now together—it had only gotten worse.

"Hold up." The voice was low and serious, causing Jordyn to stop in her tracks. "I have another question for you, Jordyn."

Jordyn stopped walking but didn't turn around. The grave and serious tone of his voice caused her heart to pound, drowning out the sound of his boots as he approached.

"This afternoon, when Adam fell onto the fence, you asked me if I had my medic bag."

Jordyn felt a jolt of adrenalin but managed to hide it. "So?"

"How did you know I was a medic?" He stood in front of her with his hands on his hips. There was no escaping the intensity of his gaze.

Jordyn changed her focus to the door over his shoulder. "I don't know." She shrugged and started to walk around him. "Mom told me, I guess. What's the big deal?"

"The big deal is that no one around here knows what I did in the service." He put his hand on her arm to stop her and leaned closer. "No. One."

The roaring in her ears became louder, but Jordyn successfully suppressed any outward reaction. "Chad, you're making a mountain out of a molehill. I wasn't asking for *your* medical bag. I just asked if you had a medical bag in the barn or something for emergencies. I didn't mean anything by it."

That caused him to pause. He cocked and his head and seemed to be replaying the event in his head, trying to remember her exact words. "No. You said, 'get *your* medic bag.'"

"No." Jordyn shook her head decisively, and then changed her mind. "Well, maybe I did. I was a little distraught at the time. But I simply meant to grab an emergency kit." She didn't look him in the eyes when she spoke. She couldn't. But after a long silence, she did finally turn her gaze to his.

"Why would the fact that you were a medic be a secret? You should be proud of your service."

He put his hand to his temple and then squeezed his eyes. "It's not a secret. I just haven't told anyone. There was never any reason to, because it's no big deal."

Jordyn was about to disagree with that statement when a voice sounded from outside the barn. "Chad? Are you in there?"

The door slid open and a woman stepped in, wearing a low-cut green dress and a coat of a slightly darker shade. She paused a moment as her eyes grew accustomed to the dim light, but she smiled broadly when she spotted Chad. The smile disappeared when her gaze shifted to Jordyn.

"What are *you* doing here?" The question was followed by a nervous laugh. "I mean, welcome back, Jordyn. I didn't know you were expected home for the holidays."

"Hi Trixie. I just got in yesterday. Nice to see you." Jordyn managed to get the last few words out without them sounding too forced. "Sorry I can't visit, but I need to get to the party to help Mom."

She didn't wait for either of them to answer, but slipped out into the cold winter air.

Chapter 12

For Christmas is tradition time—Traditions that recall the precious memories down the years, the sameness of them all.

– Helen Lowrie Marshall

As she reached for the door to the Lodge, Jordyn glanced back at the barn she'd just left, and winced at her own stupidity. Now she knew why Chad was so distant and preoccupied. Why had she assumed he was single and free? Just because he wasn't wearing a ring didn't mean he wasn't involved with someone.

Then again, Trixie was the last person she thought Chad would be interested in. Yes, she was attractive and had a figure that made men look twice, but she'd already been married twice that Jordyn knew of. What in the world could Chad possibly see in her?

But as soon as Jordyn stepped through the door, all of those thoughts vanished. A wave of emotion surged at the sound of sleigh bells, bringing back a flood of memories from Christmases past. Her father had placed a pine swag with sleigh bells on the door of the Lodge after watching the movie *It's a Wonderful Life*. But instead of an angel getting its wings when a bell chimed, he claimed that the ringing of a sleigh bell in Montana meant that a Christmas miracle was happening somewhere.

The pine swags on doors at Christmas became a family tradition and then a well-known legend throughout the region. Now everyone had them, and a few local charities depended on the money they raised at Christmas by making and selling the unique gifts to people from all over the world.

Jordyn stopped and took in the sight of the Lodge, one of her father's proudest achievements. This was the "great room" as everyone called it—an expansive community room for hosting parties or teaching classes. Through the double doors and down a long hallway on the other side of the building was a restaurant-type space where most of the guests took their meals.

The great room hadn't changed much, except that it seemed even larger than she remembered—and certainly more festive and welcoming. Two enormous stone fireplaces on each side of the cavernous space crackled and spit, throwing flickering light on the cluster of couches and chairs in front of them. The gigantic logs were blazing away now, but they would be allowed to burn down as the evening wore on so that guests could roast chestnuts. The smell would permeate the room and was a memory branded in Jordyn's mind as associated with Christmas.

Jordyn watched some volunteers put finishing touches on decorations, laughing like gleeful children as they shared a joke. They'd done a good job of capturing her father's vision for the room. Everything reflected warm Western hospitality and a cheerful holiday spirit that would make everyone feel welcome. One big family. That was his goal. It wasn't enough for him to have a structure for people to gather. He wanted the opportunity to connect lives, deepen friendships, and ensure that everyone shared in the wonder of the Christmas.

Jordyn's heart soared and sank at the same time. She was elated that her father's legacy lived on, but was sad that he wasn't here to experience it. She couldn't help but feel his spirit, his generosity, and his love permeating the room. From the cowboy-style holiday stockings hanging on the mantle, to the strategically placed mistletoe for those who wanted to grab a kiss, his passion for Christmas was everywhere she looked.

The sound of a piano attracted Jordyn's attention, and a slow smile spread across her face. This is where everyone would gather around throughout the night to sing Christmas songs and favorite hymns. The Cowboy Carolers, a group started by her father more than a dozen years earlier, would lead the chorus of amateur singers made up of the guests who cared to join in the fun.

Otherwise most of the music would be provided by a regular old-fashioned record player hooked up to a sound system. Jordyn's father loved the crackling sound it made as it played old-time Christmas classics. And the antique contraption never failed to entertain children who were enthralled by the spinning discs of vinyl.

As she soaked up the nostalgic feelings of Christmases past, Jordyn noticed the oversized manger scene to her right, which elicited another wave of memories. The handmade wooden set was her father's pride and joy, right down to the prism that hung in the window, casting a dazzling beam over the scene by day. A perfectly aimed light beam created the same effect at night.

Mr. Dunaway loved all the trimmings and excitement that came with the holiday season, but he also wanted the children to understand the true meaning of Christmas. Jordyn could picture him bending down low to explain the birth of Jesus to a group of children. He always ended by telling them that Jesus wasn't the one putting the gifts under the tree, but it was His spirit that flowed into the hearts of those who gave freely without expectation. "Every time you spread joy, love, and light," he told them, "you are celebrating the birth of Jesus and the true meaning of Christmas."

Jordyn sighed and gazed around the room. Her father wasn't here to put presents under the tree this year, but she could still feel his spirit at work, instilling joy and spreading his love. The sensation that he was near gave her an overwhelming feeling of peace and comfort that she hadn't felt for a long time.

Mrs. Dunaway appeared from the kitchen area just then, carrying a tray of wine glasses, which she placed on a small table. "Oh, you're back from the barn. Do you want to be the bartender tonight?"

Without hesitating, Jordyn nodded. "Sure. Let me get rid of these boots." Jordyn knew that being given the title of bartender was a way for her to have a job without having much to do. With this crowd, there would be more consumption of hot chocolate and eggnog than wine and cocktails.

She hurriedly pulled off the boots she'd slid on over her pumps, and stashed them and her overcoat in a closet. "Does my hair look okay?"

"It's beautiful? How's the horse?"

"We started fluids. Chad's waiting on the vet...I guess." Jordyn glanced toward the door, secretly hoping that Chad would walk through it.

"Is something wrong?" Mrs. Dunaway had started to turn away, but she returned at the tone of her daughter's voice.

"No."

"Are you sure?"

"Well, I'm just surprised, I guess...I mean I saw Trixie Wills..."

"Where?"

"In the barn. Looking for Chad, apparently."

Her mother crossed her arms and pursed her lips. "I knew something was going on when she started hanging around here all the time. She's no good for him. My goodness, she's only been divorced for a few months!"

"Unfortunately, it's not up to us to tell Chad who's good for him." Jordyn forced a laugh as she unloaded the wine glasses from the tray. She tried to appear disinterested, but she knew her mother wouldn't fall for the pretended indifference. It was hard enough to convince herself that she didn't care. She knew she would never fool her mother.

"He's like a son to me." Mrs. Dunaway put her hand on Jordyn's shoulder. "So I have every right to be annoyed. Chad isn't the type to go for someone like Trixie."

Then she became all business. "You should have everything you need here." She nodded toward the table that would soon be overflowing with appetizers and baked goods and everything in between. "Just make sure you have fun!"

Before she could comment, Mrs. Dunaway headed back to the kitchen and the door opened again, creating another loud jingle.

"Hey, Jordyn!" Kristy's cheeks were rosy and a beautiful smile radiated from her face. "I was hoping I'd find you here. Do you need any help?"

"You're back already?" Jordyn let out a sigh of relief. "How'd everything go?"

"Really good. Thanks to you and Chad, Adam is doing fine."

"Did Luke stay with you the whole time and bring you back?"

Kristy nodded, still smiling. "Yes." She leaned forward and spoke in a whisper. "And he asked me to the Gala."

"Wow, that's nice. Funny how things work out." Jordyn concentrated on arranging the wine glasses artistically on the table. "I guess you had a lot of time to talk on the ride to the hospital."

"Yes. It's funny, because we've been passing each other for the past two weeks and saying hello, but we've never really gotten a chance to talk."

"He's not from Montana?"

"No, he's from Texas. He said he always wanted to visit Montana so he packed up his truck and took a road trip. He loves it here, and says he has no reason to go back."

"In other words, he *has* a reason to stay."

Kristy's cheeks reddened, but she ignored the comment. "And he's a perfect gentleman."

"*And* good looking," Jordyn added.

"Oh, you noticed that too?" Kristy giggled like a schoolgirl, and then leaned closer to Jordyn, and nodded toward the door. "It's like a Christmas miracle."

They both turned and looked at the sleigh bells and then laughed as Jordyn gave her a hug. "I'm so happy for you. You deserve it after all you've been through."

Kristy nodded in agreement. "I've had a hard time accepting that Brad is gone, but I think it's time to move on... Strange, but I almost feel like Brad is telling me to go for it."

She talked while staring into space, but then turned toward Jordyn. "How about you and Chad? You seeing any sparks?"

"Oh, yes. Plenty of sparks." Jordyn let out her breath in one long sigh. "But not in a good way."

"You two are too stubborn to see that you were meant for each other. You were with him all morning, right?"

"Yes—but not because he wanted to be. Anyway, I didn't come back to the ranch looking for romance. I came to relax and spend time with Mom...Goodness, I didn't even know Chad was here until this morning."

"I'm sure he was surprised to see you too. And he's not the type of guy that's just going to come right out and admit that he missed you. It's just not the way he's made."

"Maybe not, but he's in the barn right now with Trixie Wills."

"*What?*"

"You heard me." Jordyn watched all the blood drain from Kristy's face. "Wait. You knew about that too, didn't you?"

Kristy looked down before meeting Jordyn's gaze. "I knew Trixie had her eyes on Chad. I didn't know she had her claws into him yet."

"That's not a very nice thing to say."

"You know her as well as I do. She's no good for Chad."

Jordyn tried again to laugh it off. "That's what Mom said, but Chad's a full-grown man. I think he can make his own decisions on who he wants to spend time with."

"But he's been through so much…" Kristy looked away as if realizing she'd just revealed a secret. "I'm sorry. I really shouldn't be gossiping."

"What do you mean, 'he's been through so much?'" Jordyn couldn't resist herself. Her mother had said something similar. She knew more about what Chad had been doing the past ten years than she let on, but she wondered what they knew.

"I know he was in the military," she said innocently. "That's not a secret, is it?"

"He doesn't talk about his years in the service at all, but after he came home, he went through some tough times." She lowered her voice considerably even though no one was close. "He was drinking heavily from what I've heard…until your mother got him to come here."

That part was news to Jordyn, but she felt uncomfortable discussing it. She tried to put an end to the conversation. "He seems good now."

"Yes. I think he's really happy being back here." Kristy looked back at Jordyn. "How did you know he was in the military? Have you been in touch with him?"

"No." Jordyn moved a wine glass and then sat it back where it had just been. "I…umm…I guess Mom told me."

More guests came through the door just then, their loud,

jovial voices interrupting the conversation. They each carried an armload of gifts and headed for the tree as the sleigh bells jingled loudly for all to hear.

"Oh my goodness, more gifts," Kristy said. "Look at that tree."

The focal point of the room at this time of year was the fifteen-foot fir tree, decked from top to bottom with red bows and twinkling white bulbs. Hundreds of colorful packages spilled out onto the floor beneath it, along with dozens of deep-hued poinsettia plants that added an extra splash of color.

"I don't think Dad knew what he was starting when he put that giant tree up in here." Jordyn stared in wonder at the beautiful sight. Her parents had made it a custom to give a small gift to each guest—but that tradition had grown and expanded over the years. Even though each cabin was provided with a Christmas tree so families could celebrate the holiday privately, many of them enjoyed sharing presents with friends that vacationed here every year together. Some of the gifts would be opened tonight as a kickoff for the holiday. Others would wait until Christmas Eve. And then, as if by magic, Santa would arrive and this space would be overflowing again on Christmas morning.

The sight of the tree made Jordyn smile, standing as a symbol of happiness and joy that would be part of their guests' memories of Christmas for years to come. Santa would make an appearance and everyone would line up to get their photo taken with him in front of the magnificent tree.

"It's overflowing, that's for sure," Kristy said. "And it's not even Christmas Eve yet."

The sight of the gifts and the spirit of giving they signified was an uplifting sight. But both women knew that presents tied up with festive ribbons and bows were just icing on the cake compared to the deeper feelings evoked. Shawn Dunaway had made it his mission to nurture and inspire a sense of togetherness and community at his one-of-a-kind premier ranch. Every guest was made to feel pampered and loved, and more importantly, experience the feeling of being part of one big family.

"I love this time of year, don't you?" Kristy looked over at Jordyn with a dreamy look of excitement and joy. "It's so magical. Especially here at Painted Sky. You just don't know what kind of wonderful miracles are going to happen next. I think your dad knew he was onto something when he created that great tradition. It's like if you believe deeply enough, a Christmas miracle will really happen."

"It's Christmas in the heart—" Jordyn said the familiar words that Shawn Dunaway lived by, and Kristy finished the sentence with her. "...That puts Christmas in the air."

The door opened yet again and the bells jangled loudly. Both women laughed because it seemed like the people who knew the local legend seemed to open the door loudly, as if they could create a Christmas miracle by merely opening the door.

"Lots of miracles happening this year, I think," Kristy said.

Jordyn forced a smile, and tried to get herself to believe in the magic again.

Chapter 13

He who has not Christmas in his heart will never find it under a tree.
– Roy L. Smith

Jordyn was surprised how much she enjoyed herself and how many faces she recognized from earlier years. Of course, some of those faces had been teenagers when she'd last seen them and now had children of their own. Others had been parents and now had grandchildren in tow.

She lost track of time as the room continued to rock with the laughter of revelers and the joyful appeals of children to open their presents early. Around ten o'clock someone came in and announced that it was snowing hard, causing everyone to rush for the door. Sure enough, big fluffy flakes fell, landing on the spreading limbs of the tall fir tree and enveloping it in a sea of swirling motion. A hush grew over the crowd as they stared at the magnificent site, and then the majority of the crowd hurried off to their private cabins to enjoy the rest of the evening with their families.

Jordyn stood outside in the cold night air, shivering but happy. She loved to watch it snow and loved the picture it would paint the next morning when the rugged landscape would be transformed into a crystalline vista of snow-covered tree limbs and an endless sea of white. A true winter wonderland.

"If it keeps snowing like this we'll be able to build a snow-man in the morning," she heard one of the children saying as they gazed around in wonder.

Jordyn went back inside, dug her boots out of the closet and threw on her coat. "I'll be right back to help clean up," she yelled to her mother as she grabbed a handful of cookies. "Just want to check on the horse."

As she tramped her way through the snow that was now beginning to stick to the ground, she couldn't help but smile. Even if the snow was gone by tomorrow, the image of seeing all those people with smiles on their faces was something she would never forget.

Walking past the vet's truck, she slid open the door and heard the sound of two men talking in the stall. The over-powering fragrance of Trixie's flowery perfume assaulted her as soon as she entered, but she didn't see her anywhere. Jor-dyn usually loved inhaling the deep, earthy smells of the barn, but the overriding scent of roses made her wrinkle her nose instead.

When she got close enough to see inside the open door of the stall, she gasped in surprise. "What happened to *you?*"

Chad had blood all over his hands and splotched on his clothes. Her gaze swept the horse who seemed to be doing fine, and then to the veterinarian. "Nothing to worry about," he assured her. "The IV just became unattached. Luckily Chad discovered it in time and was able to fix it."

Jordyn looked at Chad again, but he had turned away and was writing something down for the folder they kept on each horse. "Doc's got him all fixed up, and he's doing fine." He nodded toward a pile of manure that had been scooped up and put in a wheelbarrow.

Jordyn nodded with relief that the horse was on its way to a full recovery, yet something had happened that neither man seemed willing to explain.

"Nice to see you again, Doc. Sorry you couldn't make it up to the Lodge." Jordyn held out her hand to the vet. "Here's a couple of cookies, but there's plenty of food left if you want to stop by."

He took one cookie and laughed. "I think I'll do that. I'd like to wish your mother a Merry Christmas since I'm here."

Jordyn offered the remaining cookies to Chad, which he accepted. "Thanks. Didn't get a chance to eat."

"I'll go get you something."

"No…I…ah, need to talk to you."

The vet zipped up his coat and picked up his bag. "Call me if anything changes. Nice to see you again, Miss Jordyn."

Chad stopped him before he left. "And you'll keep this quiet, right?"

He nodded. "Sure. Not a word."

Confused as she was, Jordyn said her goodbyes and then re-entered the stall. "What's going on?" She could see Chad was tense and had a strained look on his face.

"I only left the barn for a few minutes," he said as if to explain the answer to a question she hadn't asked.

Jordyn nodded as her mind went back to Trixie. "So?"

"When I got back, the IV was wrapped all over the place and torn out, blood everywhere."

"Things happen..." Her eyes went back to the horse. "But I thought I did a really good job of taping it to make it secure."

"You did."

Her gaze went back to his. "What are you saying?"

"I knew I wasn't going to be able to stay here all night and just watch the horse, so I brought one of our foaling cameras over." He nodded to the small, barely noticeable camera that sat on the edge of the stall between the bars. "That way I could keep an eye on her from my phone."

"So you saw her twisting herself up and got here right away." Jordyn nodded. "That's good."

"Not exactly." Chad held out the camera. "Actually, I saw this."

He punched a button and Jordyn tried to make out the blurry images. It was hard to see, but it was obvious that someone entered the stall, pulled the tubing apart and then wrapped it around the mare's neck to make it look like the horse had gotten tangled. It only took a matter of seconds.

"Who would do that? Bell would have died from blood loss if you didn't have this camera on him."

Chad's face was grim. "Look again." He started the video again, as Jordyn stared harder, trying to identify the person.

"Look closer. Right here." Chad pointed the man's neck. The color was not decipherable in the grainy black and white image, but the way it was tied and the height and movements of the man made it suddenly clear.

"The checkered bandana..."

Chad nodded. "Strikes again."

"I'll go have him pack his things and get out of here right

now." Jordyn turned to leave.

"Hold on." Chad grabbed her hand to stop her. "I was thinking the same thing, but maybe we should wait."

His touch was gentle, but affected Jordyn like a branding iron. She pulled away and then stared at her arm before raising her gaze to meet his.

"*Wait?* For what? Someone or something to get hurt or killed?"

"What if it's more than just him?" Chad asked. "And *why* is he doing this? There's something big going on here. If you just get rid of him, we may never find out who else is involved and what they're up to."

Jordyn nodded, seeing his logic, but not feeling confident about the end result.

"The fact that we know who to keep our eye on might help us get to the bottom of this."

"He's trying to hurt us," she said. "Hurt the ranch."

"Yes, I think we can agree on that. But *why?*"

Jordyn shrugged. "I don't know. Why would anyone want to hurt Mom…or ruin my father's reputation?

Chad was silent for a long moment. "You may have just hit the nail on the head."

"What are you talking about?"

"Ruin your father's reputation."

"I still don't follow."

"I guess it's probably not so much that someone wants to ruin your father's reputation. Maybe they just want to ruin the *ranch's* reputation."

"That doesn't help any. Why would they want to do that?"

"So they can buy it at a cheaper price maybe?"

Jordyn's hand went to her heart and she struggled to catch her breath as she remembered the conversation with her mother earlier.

"What's wrong?" Chad noticed the reaction.

"Nothing." Jordyn shook her head. "I mean, I guess that makes sense." She looked down and then back up, not sure how much she should tell Chad.

"Why? Have you heard something?"

Jordyn nodded, knowing she could trust him, and wanting to have his help. "Mom got a letter with an offer to buy."

"Are you kidding? Was it for a good price?"

"Under normal conditions, no. But with everything that's been going on the last six months, I actually think she's talked herself into it."

"We can't let that happen."

Jordyn glanced up at him. The tone of his voice was so confident and assertive that she felt an instant wave of relief.

"I'll tell you what we're going to do," Chad continued. "The isolation shed is empty right now."

"So?"

"It's far enough away that no one should go down there. Let's put Bell in there so that whoever did this thinks he was successful."

"You mean, let him think the horse is dead?"

"Look, only you and me and Dr. Litton know the horse is fine. Maybe someone will slip up and reveal something."

"I guess it's worth a shot."

"Can you take her?" He pulled a rope from the stall door

and hooked it to the horse's halter. "I have a few other things to do to cover our tracks."

"Sure." Jordyn took the rope and glanced in the stall. "There's enough blood in here to make someone think the worst."

"Yeah, but Doc said she's fine. We just need to let her rest and take it easy for a few days." Chad handed her the camera. "Plus, I'll be able to keep an eye on her."

"Okay. I'll set up the camera, get her settled, and then head back to the Lodge."

"Don't tell anyone," Chad warned. "Not even your mother. The less she knows the better."

Jordyn nodded but her heart sank. She didn't want to lie. She hoped with all of the excitement, her mother would forget to ask.

Chapter 14

*Christmas is not as much about open-
ing our presents as opening our hearts.*

– Janice Maeditere

When Jordyn opened her eyes the next morning, it took her a few minutes to figure out where she was and why she felt so relaxed. The room was full of shadows, but she smiled when she recognized her own bed. She had slept like a rock.

The recollection of what had transpired the night before, along with thoughts of the Gala, made her bolt out of bed. She dressed quickly and braided her hair, then glanced out the window. A light layer of snow remained from the squall the night before making everything look pristine and pure. The sun was barely up so there were no footprints to disturb the smooth peaceful blanket that went on as far as the eye could see. She loved this view from her window. The shimmering waters of a small lake lay beyond the vast, unspoiled landscape, creating a vista that seemed to go on forever.

Jordyn started to turn away, then squinted and looked again at one large scar in a far-off field that marred the unspoiled landscape. One of her father's large bulldozers sat to the side of a large mound of dirt. Puzzled, but too sleepy to be overly curious, she headed down the stairs, following the smell of freshly brewed coffee.

As predicted, Mrs. Dunaway was already busy in the kitchen, as were a number of other people working over the stove. "Grab a cup of coffee, honey," she said when she saw Jordyn. "You look like you need it."

Still sleepy-eyed, Jordyn pulled a big mug out of the cabinet. "Wasn't that snow beautiful last night?"

"Yes, everyone's talking about it." Her mother laughed. "I love seeing the children witness their first snow."

"Especially this close to Christmas." Jordyn took a big swallow of coffee and closed her eyes. "So good. Just like I remember." Then she opened her eyes wide. "Mom, it's Christmas Eve!"

Her mother looked up calmly as she kneaded dough for fresh bread. "Yes, dear. It's Christmas Eve. Lots to do."

"How can I help? Oh my goodness. The Gala is tonight! I can't believe how fast time is flying by."

"I think they have breakfast under control in the Lodge, but we're cooking for the guests who want to eat breakfast in their cabins. You could help with deliveries."

"Order for Cabin Fifteen is up," someone yelled just then.

"That sounds like a perfect job for me." Jordyn took the bag to the foyer where she pulled on a pair of cowboy boots and threw on a coat. The morning air was chilly but so fresh and clean that she delighted with each breath. She counted the cabins as she walked by and then climbed the steps to Cabin Fifteen and knocked the door. "Breakfast delivery."

The door opened to a smiling gentleman wearing sweatpants and a sweater. His wife stood behind him, wearing flannel pajamas with a red and white snowman pattern. "Sorry to be so lazy. We thought it would be fun to eat breakfast in our cabin."

Jordyn laughed. "That's what you're supposed to be doing on vacation. Taking it easy. Do you want me to put it on the table for you?"

"No, I've got it." The man took the package. "Thanks for bringing it, though."

"You're welcome. Merry Christmas!" Jordyn started to leave, but the man spoke again in a low, grave voice. "We were sorry to hear about that horse…especially so close to Christmas."

Jordyn turned around, confused. "What horse?" For a moment, she forgot all about the incident of the night before.

"The one that died."

"Oh…well—" Jordyn wasn't sure what to say.

"I've been coming here since I was a kid and love this place." He cleared his throat. "But one of the ranch hands told me that ever since Mr. Dunaway died, the horses aren't being taken care of like they used to be. I can't really believe that's true. They all seemed fat and healthy to me."

Jordyn felt her face growing red with suppressed emotion. "That's not true at all. I'd be glad to give you a private tour of the barns later. I don't think you'll find horses anywhere in Montana that are more pampered than the ones here."

"I'd love to do that," his wife said from behind him.

"She's a horse nut." The man smiled.

"Great. How about later this morning? Say ten?"

The woman nodded and laughed. "Perfect. I should be dressed by then."

"I'll stop by and pick you up." Jordyn turned to leave, but paused when she hit the top step. "Just out of curiosity, can you tell me which ranch hand said something about the horse?"

The man's brow wrinkled as if he were trying to remember a name. "It was a big guy...Jeb, maybe?" He looked back at his wife to see if she remembered. "No, I think his name was Judd. He chews tobacco." The woman made a face. "Spits it everywhere."

"Thanks and Merry Christmas." Jordyn turned to leave. "See you later for the tour."

As she headed back toward the house, Jordyn took a deep breath that reflected both satisfaction and discomfort. Chad had been right about Judd. But that didn't mean it was going to be easy to prove it.

Chapter 15

The only blind person at Christmas time is he
who has not Christmas in his heart.

– Helen Keller

Jordyn stayed busy for the next two hours delivering breakfasts. Everyone was in a cheerful mood and wanted to chat—especially about the Gala that evening. The days preceding the event were always filled with activities, but Gala day was set aside to relax, go for long walks or just stay in the snug cabins in front of the fire until it was time for the big party.

After making her last trip to the row of cabins, Jordyn started back to the house, but made a slight detour to go by the chapel her father had built. Made of stone and logs, it stood at the base of a hill and appeared as rustic and idyllic as the land itself. It was one of the first buildings he'd added and he'd done most of the work himself. It now stood as a labor of love that had withstood the testament of time. Dozens of couples had met at Painted Sky over the years and come back to say their vows in the holy spot.

The church looked like a painting or a postcard decorated for Christmas. Swags of pine adorned with red ribbons lay on each window ledge, and even though it was daytime, flickering candlelight reflected off the glass from inside. Jordyn's gaze swept the area and landed on the large stack of wood that would be set ablaze later to help illuminate the night sky. There would be numerous roaring bonfires to light the way, as well as dozens of smaller campfires with marshmallow and hot chocolate stations nearby.

It always amazed Jordyn how many women would throw on a coat and a pair of boots over their beautiful dresses to go for a walk on Christmas Eve. No matter the weather or how deep the snow, the lighted fires would lead the way through some of the most spectacular towering pine forests and night sky vistas. If the night was clear, star gazers would be enthralled by the vast, wide open sky that twinkled with an infinite number of brilliant stars.

Jordyn turned around and headed back to the house, and caught sight of the man she'd been hoping to find. "Mr. Judson." She pretended to be cheerful when she saw him standing on the porch of the ranch hand cabin. "I'm Jordyn Dunaway. I've been meaning to stop by and introduce myself. I understand you're the new foreman."

He'd been leaning on the railing, but pulled himself up to his full height, as if by doing so she wouldn't notice the thick sludge of mid-section that hung over his oversized belt buckle. "Pleased to meet you, Miss Dunaway. I've heard a lot about you." His gaze started at her eyes, but slowly perused her entire body before returning.

She almost said the same thing to him, but decided a better course of action would be to remain friendly. "It's nice to have someone taking care of things for Mom." She kept her voice calm and even despite the fact that just saying the words caused a new wave of anger to surge.

He straightened his shoulders a little more. "That's my job, ma'am. My pleasure."

Jordyn took a step closer. "I don't want to get off on the wrong foot or anything, but I just heard a complaint about your use of chewing tobacco, and—"

"From who?" he retorted angrily, looking at the row of cabins as if to figure out which one had said something. "It's none of their business."

"I didn't mean to start an argument." Jordyn kept her voice upbeat and cheerful, betraying nothing of her anger and disgust. "But I'm sure my mother told you about chewing and spitting in front of guests."

Judd's eyes narrowed and his brow creased. He opened his mouth to respond, but then apparently thought better of it. He merely smiled and lifted his hat in an exaggerated fashion. "Very well, Miss Dunaway. Thank you for the reminder."

Jordyn nodded and waved as she started to walk away. "Merry Christmas!"

"I mean, I can understand why you'd be a little on edge, seeing as how that horse died last night. It don't reflect too good on the ranch."

Jordon stopped in her tracks, but didn't turn around at first. She concentrated on his words rather than the roaring in her ears. "I beg your pardon?"

"Now don't try to hide it, Miss Dunaway." He lowered his voice as if they were confiding in one another. "I know all about Bell."

"What about her?" Jordyn turned now and took a step closer. "I mean, yes, she was sick and the vet came. But she was fine when I left the barn last night." She took a deep breath of satisfaction that her voice hadn't trembled in the least.

"You mean Chad didn't tell you?" Judd's face lit up as if it brought him great pleasure to be able to break the bad news to her himself.

"Tell me what?"

"That the horse got tangled up and ripped the IV out. Bled to death, apparently."

"No. That can't be true." Jordyn put her hand over her mouth, feigning surprise.

"Sorry to break it to you." He pointed to the bulldozer up on the hill. "What do you think that's for? Chad took that thing out there in the middle of the night and dug the hole. Right on the other side of the hill I guess so no one would see or hear."

Jordyn almost burst out laughing, but successfully resisted the urge. When Chad said he had other things to do, she hadn't known what he'd meant. But it all made sense now. If a horse had died, they would either need to produce a body or a grave to make it believable. He'd gone the extra mile to make it look like a horse had been buried on the property.

"I'm surprised he didn't tell you." Judd said, as he eyed her with a calculating expression. "Maybe he's trying to cover up his own incompetence."

Jordyn put her face in her hands. "I can't believe it. Not Bell." She peered at him through her fingers. "How do you know what happened? Did you find her?"

"No. The bad thing is, it was one of the guests...so it probably won't be kept quiet for very long." Judd tilted his head as if assessing how she would take that news.

"Oh, no. Which one? Maybe I should have a talk with him...ask him to keep it quiet."

"You can try, I guess." Judd crossed his arms across his barrel chest. "His first name is Ricky. That's all I know."

"Does he wear a black checkered bandana?"

"Yeah, that's the one." He leaned forward with squinty eyes. "How'd you know?"

"I heard him introduce himself to someone." Jordyn quickly tried to cover her mistake, and then tried to dive for more information. "What did he do when he found her? That's so terrible."

"Well, of course he ran out and tried to find someone to help. I was the first person he ran into since everyone else was still at the Lodge celebrating and enjoying their holiday."

Jordyn didn't need to ask the next question on her lips.

"But before I could get over there, I saw Chad heading into the barn, so I decided to just let him handle it. There was nothing that could be done according to what Ricky said."

"It's so sad." Jordyn wiped away a make-believe tear. "Thanks for telling me."

Chapter 16

*Christmas is most truly Christmas when we celebrate it
by giving the light of love to those who need it most.*

– Ruth Carter Stapleton

Jordyn made her way back to the house, hoping she would run into Chad. The ranch was a beehive of activity now with everyone having a job to do—either making sure the guests were having a good time, or preparing for the Gala that was set to kick off in mere hours.

It wasn't until much later in the morning that Jordyn caught a glimpse of the man she'd been wishing to find. She'd just finished giving the private tour to the couple in the cabin and was walking back toward the barn. With a smile on her face, she walked over to the small corral and leaned her arms on the top rail of the fence.

"Howdy, cowboy," she said to the young boy who sat in the saddle in front of Chad as they walked by her.

"I'm riding! I'm riding!" The boy's smile was so big and his face was so bright, she wished her father could be here to witness the scene. Yet, in a way, he was. She could feel his spirit taking part in the Christmas magic he'd helped create.

Jordyn knew there was no such ride on the schedule, and that Chad had a thousand other things to get done today. But he must have noticed the wishful look in the young boy's eyes and offered him a ride. That was Chad. Fearless and charming. Gentle and tough. Kind and charismatic.

Turning her head, Jordyn noticed the boy's parents standing near the gate beside an empty wheelchair. Their faces were beaming almost as brightly as their son's, although they both seemed to be brushing away tears. "I'll open the gate if you want to get some pictures," Jordyn said to the parents.

"Yes. Please! We can't believe he's *riding* a horse. We didn't even think he would touch one."

Jordyn led them into the center of the ring, as Chad asked, "Ready to go a little faster?"

When the boy nodded enthusiastically, he urged the horse into a slow trot and then a gentle lope. The boy squealed with pure delight as Chad held him firmly in the saddle with one strong arm, while the other hand guided the horse around the enclosure.

Finally, Chad handed the reins to the boy and let him pull the horse to a stop. "Good job," Chad told him. "You'll be a regular cowboy in no time."

In that moment, Jordyn understood what the Grinch felt when his heart grew three sizes that day—only hers seemed to be melting. To see the robust, muscular man in the saddle put everything aside to give this family a few minutes of joy, almost brought her to tears as well. Chad wasn't the type of man to show emotion, yet his gentle and generous spirit was too strong to be hidden.

As the parents went up to greet their son, Jordyn offered to take family pictures in front of the horse, which they enthusiastically accepted. Chad was the only one who disagreed.

"I'll dismount and stand on the other side."

"No. We want you in the picture," the boy's mother insisted.

Jordyn snapped picture after picture, until at last the father walked back to the gate to get the wheelchair. Jordyn held the boy in the saddle as Chad dismounted, then he effortlessly lifted the boy and placed him back in his chair.

"I don't know how to thank you for this." The mother threw her arms around Chad with tears flowing down her cheek.

"It was my pleasure, ma'am. Merry Christmas." He tipped his hat courteously, but looked extremely uncomfortable.

The father stood beside Jordyn and leaned close. "You probably don't know this, but he's never talked before."

Jordyn's gaze darted over to his as she recalled the boy telling her that he was riding. "But he—"

The man nodded, and now he had tears in his eyes too. "If I had known that all I had to do was take him to Painted Sky Ranch, I would have done it years ago."

Jordyn swiped a tear from her own eye as she thought once again about her father. His dreams really had turned to reality. Thanks to Chad, this ranch had truly conveyed something tangible and perceptible. Some might even call it Christmas magic. She wished everyone could experience this heartwarming feeling and understand how a simple act of kindness could change someone's life so drastically.

Jordyn watched Chad walk away, his head bent down against a strong north wind, his leather chaps making a familiar flapping sound that had once been so familiar to her. His figure exemplified power, fortitude, an innate inner calm, causing her to realize how gentle and kind a truly strong man could be.

Memories and recollections of her earlier years with Chad came flooding back, along with a new revelation.

Chad had not only been her first love.

He was her *only* love.

Chapter 17

Gifts of time and love are surely the basic ingredients of a truly merry Christmas.

– Peg Bracken

After Jordyn had said her own goodbyes to the couple, she headed for the barn and found Chad already busy at work in the tack room.

"I have some news," she said.

He continued cleaning a bridle without looking up. "So do I. Go ahead."

"Judd is definitely in on it."

She watched the brim of his hat slowly rise as he met her gaze.

"How do you know?"

"He told me Bell was dead. He showed me the bulldozer as proof." She smiled and gave him a compliment. "Nice touch."

He met the statement with a blank stare. "So the bandana guy is working for Judd, and Judd is working for the McClatchy Group."

"*What?*" Jordyn thought back to where she'd heard the name. "The McClatchy Group is the corporation that wants to buy the ranch."

"That figures." Chad shoved his hat off his brow a little.

"I did some research last night, called some friends who still live in the area. They said the McClatchy Group bought the Bowden and Carlton ranches over the past three years."

"The Carlton Ranch borders us to the South."

"And the Bowden Ranch borders you to the North. Painted Sky is right in the middle and it's the only one of the three that has frontage on the river."

"If someone wants it, why don't they just make a legitimate offer?"

"Probably because they know its value is much higher than what they're able to pay. Plus, they must have assumed that your mother is vulnerable. She's got her hands full and she's getting older. They probably figured if they could just pile things up right at the most stressful time of the year, she'd throw her hands up and sell."

"What a terrible thing to do...and at Christmas no less." Jordyn put her hands on her hips. "How do we prove that and get rid of him?"

"I've been trying to figure that out."

"Well, you have Ricky, the bandana guy on tape. All we have to do is link the two of them."

"I may have already done that." Chad looked up.

"How?"

He pulled a piece of paper out of his pocket. "I was going over some paperwork, and thought it was a little strange that Judd would volunteer to go pick up one of the guests at the airport."

Jordyn cocked her head and looked at him with confused eyes. "Ricky?"

He nodded. "That made me even more suspicious, so I had a good friend of mine do some digging."

"Is that legal?""

"He's a private investigator. Everything he found is public information."

"And?"

"Believe it or not, the last known employer of both men was the McClatchy Group—and neither one has an end date."

"So you're saying, they still work for them?"

"That's what the paper trail suggests."

"Let's go look at Mom's contract with Judd. The information you found should provide a sound reason for dismissal."

They started walking toward the house, but Jordyn pulled Chad to a stop when they got to the porch. "I want to thank you again, Chad. I don't know what I'd do if you weren't here."

He stared at her a moment as if trying to figure out what to say. "That's what friends are for, right?" He turned and kept on walking.

Jordyn wasn't sure if she should be glad he considered her a friend again…or disappointed they weren't more than that. Yes, ten years had passed, but she felt as comfortable with him now as she had the day she'd left. She trusted him. She admired him. And she respected him more than any man she'd ever met other than her father.

She wished he could forgive her, forget the rift between them, and at least *try* to go back to the way it was.

By the time he pushed open the door, Jordyn came to her senses and realized there were more important things to take care of than a broken relationship. Her mother happened to be walking by and stopped as they entered.

"What are you two up to?" Her worried gaze darted back and forth between them, as if trying to determine if they brought good news or bad.

"We think we might have an answer to your dilemma," Jordyn said.

"You told Chad?"

"Some of it. He guessed the rest."

"We'd like to see the contract you have with Judd, Mrs. Dunaway." Chad had his hat in his hand, and was wiping his feet before entering.

Mrs. Dunaway started walking toward the office. "You're welcome to look at it, but I already told Jordyn, it's ironclad. My lawyer told me I needed justification to let him go."

"What if he already works for someone else? Would that be justification?"

Mrs. Dunaway stopped walking and turned around. "What are you talking about?"

"He's employed by the McClatchy Group."

"But that's who I got the letter from." Mrs. Dunaway appeared both confused and angry.

"That's a bit of a conflict of interest, don't you think?"

"Yes, I'd say so." Mrs. Dunaway entered the office and sat down at the desk. She opened a drawer and pulled out a folder. "Here it is, but my attorney told me that firing him because I don't like the job he's doing is not adequate cause under Montana law."

"He was probably right about that," Chad said. "Montana is the only state that protects employees to this extent."

"Yes, that's what the lawyer told me," Mrs. Dunaway said. "Something about the Montana Wrongful Discharge from Employment Act."

"Right. But if we can now prove that he is actually employed by someone who is trying to purchase your ranch, I think that will fall under a lawful termination."

"What about Ricky?" Jordyn reminded Chad that it wasn't just Judd they had to worry about.

"Who's Ricky?" Mrs. Dunaway asked.

"He's one of the guests. But he's here under false pretenses, too." Jordyn didn't go into the fact that he'd almost killed a horse in order to convince her to sell."

"I think we should call the police," Chad said. "And then I'm going to go have a talk with both Ricky and Judd."

"No. I'm not sure you should do that." Mrs. Dunaway shook her head. "Judd will put up a fight. I know he will. It's Christmas Eve. I don't want to cause a scene. It will look *terrible*."

"Don't worry. I'll talk to them in such a way that they'll be happy to quietly pack their bags and get out of here without being in handcuffs.

"You're going to just let them go?" Jordyn asked.

"I didn't say that." Chad spoke with a slight smile on his face, but he didn't expound upon what he meant.

"I don't know what I'd do without you two here." Mrs. Dunaway threw her arms around both of them. "I'm so lucky to have you both here."

Chad returned the hug with one arm, and wrapped the other one around Jordyn, causing a lump to rise in her throat.

Jordyn felt pretty lucky herself at that moment to be holding onto the two people she loved most in the world. Not only that, but it was Christmas Eve and she was *home*. A sense of bottomless peace and contentment seized her making Jordyn feel blissfully happy and fully alive.

When Mrs. Dunaway finally pulled away, she wiped a tear from her cheek. "But how are you going to get them to leave without causing a scene?"

"Don't worry Mrs. Dunaway," Chad said, turning toward the door. "I have a plan."

Chapter 18

*If you haven't got any charity in your heart, you
have the worst kind of heart trouble.*

– Bob Hope

C had stood quietly behind a pine tree about fifty feet
away from the ranch manager's cabin, while staring
at the screen on his phone. Ricky had just arrived and
was talking to Judd on the porch.

The conversation was taking place just out of earshot, but
Chad watched Ricky reach into his back pocket and pull out
a slip of paper. He waved it in the air and pointed to it as he
questioned Judd as to what it was about.

As predicted, Judd was shaking his head confusedly. He
didn't know anything about the note requesting Ricky to come
to his cabin because he hadn't written it. Chad had.

It was all part of the plan.

Everything was running right on schedule, including the
slow advance of Jordyn from the isolation barn over the hill.
She was riding Bell bareback with her legs dangling in a relaxed manner. The two men didn't even notice her until she
smiled and waved. "Look what I found. Isn't it wonderful? A
Christmas miracle!"

The two men standing on the porch didn't seem to think so.

Chad turned up the volume on his phone as their gazes went from Jordyn, to the horse, and then to each other. When she had disappeared from sight, Judd's hands tightened into fists. "Isn't that the horse you told me was *dead*?"

Ricky stared blankly in the direction where the horse and rider had since disappeared. He seemed stunned, as if he didn't quite believe what his eyes were telling him. "There's no way..."

"There's no way? But you just saw her! And she looked *fine*."

"But I pulled the plug on the catheter just like you told me to. And I watched the blood dripping out. No, it can't be..."

"It was Chad, I bet." Judd talked as if to himself. "Trixie didn't keep him occupied long enough. He must have gone in there and reattached it."

Chad's head shot up at that. So Trixie was in on this too. He hadn't considered that possibility, even though he'd been suspicious of her appearance and her sudden need for him to take a look at a warning light in her car.

"What are we going to do?" Ricky crossed his arms. "We've lost a lot of leverage without having a dead horse. She'll never sell this place unless she's desperate. I've already started spreading rumors that they ain't taking care of their horses, but without any evidence, no one's going to believe it. Those horses are better fed than I am half the time."

"Darn it." Judd took his hat off and hit the side of his leg with it. "You bungled this big-time and now Chad is probably onto us."

"What do you mean?"

"He pretended the horse was dead to see what we would do, didn't he?"

"But he doesn't really know what's going on." Ricky sounded confident. "He might suspect something. But he ain't that smart."

"I don't know about that." Judd shook his head. "He don't like me. I can tell. I think he knows that all the little things going on around here started when I arrived. He's smart enough to know that's no coincidence."

Chad took that as his cue and started to whistle as he walked closer to the cabin. The men stopped talking immediately, but he pretended not to notice. "Merry Christmas." He smiled and waved.

"Yeah, ahh, Merry Christmas," Judd mumbled, slightly flustered at his sudden appearance.

"You two look like you're having a serious conversation." Chad came to a stop in front of them as if he just happened to be walking by.

"No. Just talking about what a wonderful day it is."

"It is a wonderful day, isn't it?" Chad turned toward them and started walking up the steps. "That reminds me...I left something here that I need to grab." He reached up near the top of the post and removed the foaling camera he had placed there earlier. "I'll just get this out of your way."

Both men stood with their mouths open as they obviously tried to replay in their minds what they had just said and how damaging it would be. Judd reacted almost immediately by making a wild grab toward the camera, but Chad pulled it out of his reach. "Just so you know, everything recorded on here has been automatically downloaded to my phone."

"This ain't legal. You can't do this." Judd recovered enough to put up a fight. "I got lawyers and we'll fight this! You don't know who you're dealing with."

"You're on private property and were recorded on a security camera," Chad replied calmly. "I'll give you the number for the ranch's attorneys and you can discuss who broke the law. Okay?"

As expected, Judd didn't back down. He shook his finger at Chad, and bellowed in a voice that could be heard for quite a distance. "Do what you want, but I'll make sure this ranch's reputation is destroyed." He glanced at his watch. "That's right. The big Gala is about to begin and I'm going to make sure everyone hears about this."

"Actually, here's what's going to happen." Chad's voice was low but confident, an intimidating combination. "I have enough evidence on here to put you in jail for a long time, but I'm going to give you both the opportunity to leave with your heads up. All you have to do is pack your bags and vacate this property…immediately and quietly."

He paused a moment to let that sink in. "But if you're not off this land in the next thirty minutes, the police will be here to remove you. Leave peacefully. Or leave in handcuffs. The choice is yours." He crossed his arms and eyed both men intently as they stood without speaking.

"Do you *understand?*" Chad's voice grew loud.

Both men nodded their heads, but they seemed so stunned by how quickly the tables had been turned they were unable to move.

"The clock is running." He glanced at his watch. "You only have twenty-nine more minutes."

That caused them to move, one going one way and one the other. "Make sure you warn Trixie," he shouted after them. "Don't forget, you mentioned her on the video too."

When both men had disappeared, Chad made his way to the barn. He found Jordyn in Bell's stall, hanging up a bucket of water. "They're packing now," he told her. "I expect they'll be off the property in the next fifteen minutes."

"Then what? They're just going to get away with it?

"Then it's out of our hands." He crossed his arms and leaned against the stall door. "Except that I've already sent all the information to the police, and they probably have officers ready to pull them over as soon as they hit the main road."

Jordyn surprised him by throwing her arms around his neck. "Chad, thank you so much! What would I do without you?"

"I don't know, Jordyn." He unwrapped himself from her embrace and stepped away. "But you seem to have figured that out just fine over the past ten years."

Chapter 19

Some Christmas tree ornaments do more than glitter and glow, they represent a gift of love given a long time ago.
– Tom Baker

"Any good news about Chad?" Kristy asked the question while using a curling iron on her hair. She looked innocently toward Jordyn as if the question had just popped into her head, but Jordyn knew she'd been dying to ask it all evening.

Jordyn didn't answer right away. She leaned closer to the mirror they were sharing and turned her head from side to side, checking out the small silver and red beads that Kristy had braided into her hair. The result was a festive holiday look that looked both sophisticated and glamorous.

"No." She didn't bother to tell Kristy his last words to her, and how much they had stung. They still hurt too much to repeat them, and she winced just thinking about it.

"But he's coming to the Gala, right?" Kristy put the curling iron down and picked up a brush.

The two of them had decided to do their makeup and hair in a huge dressing room in the Lodge, just like the old days. Jordyn had been enjoying laughing and catching up with her best friend. The last ten years had melted away as if they'd never been apart, but now Jordyn felt a hint of wariness. She didn't want anyone to see how intensely she felt about Chad.

"Maybe at some point." Jordyn leaned forward, trying to act indifferent as she put on a light shade of lipstick. "Mom said he's helping to deliver wood."

"Oh, I guess it's all hands on deck to be a wood elf to-night." Kristy laughed. "I almost forgot about that tradition."

"Me too. Every other day of the year it's up to the guests to get their own wood, but tonight it gets delivered."

"Your father was so creative. It's those little things that make Painted Sky so special to everyone."

Jordyn smiled. "Dad and I used to do it ourselves though—and in the middle of the night, so when people woke up on Christmas day they would discover the 'wood elves' had come. Now there are too many cabins, so everyone pitches in."

"How do I look?" Kristy twirled around in her green and red dress, making it swirl out around her, as they prepared to make their way out to the party.

"You look like you'll turn every head in the room," Jordyn said as they walked down the hallway. "Luke is a lucky man."

"Aww. Thanks. I can't believe I'm this excited—and nervous." Kristy held her hand over heart. "I haven't gone on a date—or even thought of such a thing—for years."

"You're going to have a great time," Jordyn said. "Luke seems like a really nice guy."

The sound of music playing and lots of talking and laughing reached their ears a few moments before Jordyn opened the door.

"Does your mother have you doing anything special?"

Kristy asked as her eyes searched the room full of people. Some were dressed in gowns and tuxes, and some were dressed in blue jeans and cowboy hats. But it was plain to see that everyone in attendance was already in high spirits.

"She gave me strict orders to 'mingle' and enjoy myself. That's all." Jordyn gave Kristy a quick hug as she saw Luke waving at her from the other side of the room. "Merry Christmas! Have a great time."

Kristy had no sooner left her side when someone from town recognized Jordyn and began chattering away. For the next few hours that scene repeated itself over and over as old friends from high school or people who knew her father gave her a hug and talked as if there had never been an absence of a decade. She also chatted with families who had been coming to Painted Sky for years, and appreciated hearing stories about her father that she'd never heard before.

But she couldn't help but occasionally search the crowd for Chad's tan cowboy hat. If nothing else, she wanted to thank him again for getting rid of Judd and Ricky. That action had lifted her mother's spirits noticeably and relieved her of a huge amount of stress. His plan had worked like a charm, with none of the guests—or apparently even the ranch hands—noticing the two missing men. One of the volunteers had noticed Trixie was missing though because she'd signed up to help. Another had said he'd seen her leave in a hurry without saying goodbye.

Jordyn grabbed a cup of hot chocolate from the table and did a doubletake when she noticed Chad standing by one of the fireplaces. There was an air of isolation about his tall figure, yet his appearance was compelling. He turned to throw another piece of wood on the blaze, but the person beside him continued to converse as if trying to keep his attention. Jordyn recognized the woman instantly. The red cowboy hat and boots from the trail ride had been replaced with a bright red shimmering gown…and matching red lips.

The wannabe cowgirl was conspicuous, but then again, Chad was quite noticeable too. Clean-shaven and sporting a nice red shirt of his own, he stood out…a massive, self-confident presence in a room filled to the brim with handsome cowboys. No wonder Miss Red Dress had latched onto him.

Jordyn watched as the two of them stood shoulder to shoulder while the woman showed Chad something on her phone. His eyes grew large and expressive as she flipped through the screens with long, red fingernails.

Jordyn tried to ignore the feelings of jealously that surged through her when she saw Chad leave her side, and then return within a few minutes with a glass of wine. Was he just being nice? Or was he actually enjoying her company? His last words to her replayed once again in her mind, making her cheeks feel warm with remorse and regret.

Seeming to sense her eyes upon him, Chad glanced up and offered her a distracted nod, the type of polite moving of the head that might come from an uninterested stranger. Jordyn raised her chin and assumed all the dignity she could muster before turning away and engaging in conversation with a guest.

Though she tried to enjoy herself for the next forty-five minutes, Jordyn was glad when she noticed a large number of empty mugs beginning to pile up on the front table. Loading them onto a tray hidden under the table, she headed toward the kitchen. She needed some time to think. To breathe.

When she was almost to the swinging door, Chad stepped in front of her. "Let me take that. It looks heavy."

"I've got it," Jordyn snapped in response. "Go enjoy Miss Red Dress."

"Whoa." He ignored her and lifted the tray out of her hands, a crooked smile peeking through his usually straight face. "I didn't know you were watching me that closely."

"I wasn't *watching* you." Jordyn attempted to cover her mistake while trying to keep her heart cold and still. "I just noticed you talking to her, that's all."

Chad continued into the kitchen and set the tray down on the counter beside the sink. Jordyn ignored him as she began placing the glasses in the dishwasher one by one.

"The strange thing is, she's a photographer," he said as if just making conversation.

"Really?" Jordyn snorted. "Because I've never seen her with a camera."

"I've never seen you with one either, to tell you the truth."

Jordyn froze, but only for a moment. "I'm on vacation. No one does their professional work when they're on vacation."

"That's what *she* said." Chad found a plate of vegetables on the center island and gnawed on a celery stick, as he stared thoughtfully at the reflection of blinking Christmas lights through the window. "Taking pictures is the *last* thing she wants to do when she's here to relax."

"And what's the *first* thing? Hooking up with a cowboy?"

Jordyn regretted the words as soon as they were spoken.

Chad cocked his head and looked over at her. "You sound jealous."

"Why would I be jealous?" Jordyn took the last glass from the tray and sat it down on the counter with a loud bang.

"Easy with that." Chad crossed his arms and his legs, and leaned back against the counter, studying her with his head tilted to the side. "It's funny, with her being a photographer and all, that she's never heard of you."

Jordyn's breath caught in her throat as she began to understand what this conversation was about, and why he had offered to help her in the first place. She could tell he was puzzled…could almost see the wheels of his mind spinning. He was beginning to question if the job she'd been doing and the job everyone thought she'd been doing were two different things.

She recovered quickly and said the first thing that came to her mind. "That's probably because she's an international floozy who pretends to be a photographer so she can latch on to a *gullible* cowboy."

"No, I don't think so."

Jordyn turned her gaze to Chad at the seriousness of his tone. That's when she noticed the bolo he was wearing. Made of silver and engraved with the image of a horseshoe, it was both familiar and memorable. "Is that Dad's?" she asked raising her gaze to meet his.

Chad looked confused at the sudden change of conversation, then realized what she was talking about. "Yes. Your mother let me borrow it. I don't have one anymore."

Jordyn continued to stare at the familiar piece that her father had called his lucky charm, but Chad went back to the conversation at hand. "Anyway, she showed me some of her photos from magazines on her phone. Pretty impressive. And if she can afford to stay here for Christmas, she must be doing pretty well for herself, right?"

"What exactly are trying to get at, Chad?" Jordyn didn't really want to spend the rest of her evening talking about the woman in the red dress. "Just spit it out."

Chad opened a can of soda, poured it into a glass, and then regarded her thoughtfully. His deliberate, casual attitude came across as boldly intimating, and when he leaned back and sipped the drink slowly, Jordyn felt a wave of panic.

"Like I said, she's never heard of you. I just find it a little strange considering the fact that you've been traveling around the world for the past ten years in the exact same profession."

Jordyn felt impaled by his steady gaze as a tense silence enveloped the room. She swallowed hard, not sure how to respond.

"And then there's the snake, and about a dozen other things that just aren't adding up. So I guess what I'm getting at is..." He leaned forward, his eyes clinging to hers as if analyzing her reaction. "What are you hiding?"

Jordyn was so stunned by the suddenness of the question she didn't know what to say. The minute she'd seen Chad, she'd known in her heart this moment was going to come—but not so abruptly and from out of the blue. She bit her lip and looked away, shaking her head as she tried to untangle the jumbled thoughts that left her unable to come up with a reasonable response.

"I'm sorry, Chad. I never meant to leave you like that." She shook her head and looked down, knowing that sounded like a weak excuse. "I never meant to hurt you."

"And let me guess," he retorted angrily. "You never meant to lie."

Jordyn closed her eyes and prayed, asking for guidance on how to respond. He was right. She'd never meant to lie. And especially not to him. But the truth was just as hard to explain—and certainly more complicated—than the lie had been.

She moistened her dry lips nervously as a flicker of foreboding coursed through her. She'd once been good at masking her inner turmoil with deceptive calm—but under his steady scrutiny she felt incapable of pretending.

"*Terra Gardez.*" The name of the far-away town tumbled out though she'd had no intention of revealing this long-held secret.

Chad nearly choked on the soda he'd just swallowed. "Excuse me? What do you know about *Terra Gardez*?"

Jordyn paused, not sure she should continue, then plunged right ahead. "I was there." She took a deep breath, enjoying the feeling of relief the admission brought even though she'd not made the decision to confess it to him consciously. The sudden disclosure had been dredged from a place beyond logic or reason.

"That's not funny. Stop playing around, Jordyn." The calm expression on Chad's face was replaced with raw emotion. "You couldn't have been there. It was me and three other guys on a rescue op, and one of them didn't make it out alive."

Jordyn didn't say anything. She couldn't. She closed her eyes as guilt and grief consumed her—even though she knew it wasn't her fault.

Chad's voice interrupted her thoughts. "The only way you could have been there is if—"

She opened her eyes as his gaze darted back to her again.

She nodded, trying to keep her own emotions under stern restraint. "You saved my life. I didn't know it at the time, but—"

He shook his head, obviously replaying the memory in his head. "No. It couldn't have been you. The woman had dark hair…and she definitely wasn't a photographer." He flung the word out as if it were poison. "She was an intelligence officer…the only survivor on a military chopper that went down in enemy territory. Our mission was to rescue her."

Jordyn merely nodded as she thought about how unrecognizable she'd been. Her hair had been dyed black and she'd been pretty banged up. When she woke up in the field hospital after the rescue, her face was so swollen and her eyes so black and blue that she didn't even recognize herself.

Chad's eyes remained fixed on the wall over her shoulder, as a wistfulness stole into his expression. She saw a nerve in his cheek flick indicating things were beginning to fall into place. The long absences without word to her family. The secrets. The lies. She watched the play of emotions on his face as he turned his steady eyes to her. "Who are you Jordyn Dunaway?"

The door to the kitchen burst open just then and Mrs.

Dunaway came hurrying in. "I was afraid I'd find you in here working instead of enjoying the party." She motioned to Jordyn and then noticed Chad. "You too? Come on! It's time for the sing-along!"

As Jordyn followed her mother through the door, she felt Chad's hand clasp hers and pull her to a stop. His touch was strong. Firm. Protective. Her heart thumped violently in her throat, but Jordyn didn't say anything. She turned and looked up at him, afraid of what she would see. Distrust? Disbelief? Disapproval?

It was none of the above. His look conveyed thoughtfulness, not judgment.

"Let's talk. *Now.* Just you and me."

Chapter 20

The Christmas spirit is a spirit of giving and forgiving.

– James Cash Penney

Jordyn nodded once and then made her way to the closet for her boots and a coat. There was an inch of snow on the ground and more falling heavily, but neither one of them really seemed aware of it.

The night was quiet until the sound of their breaths as they labored to climb the hill broke the stillness. Without warning Chad pulled her down on a bench beside him next to a small crackling campfire. "Why didn't you tell me?" His voice sounded more disappointed than angry. "I would have understood about the job if you would have just told me."

Jordyn blinked back tears that appeared out of nowhere. "I did actually try…that night before I left." She looked down at her idle hands. "But you told me to 'just go.' You said you didn't really care one way or the other."

"No!" Chad shook his head. "I mean…well…maybe I did." He rubbed his hand over his chin in agitation. "I thought I was going to spend the rest of my life with you, and you turned around and told me you were leaving. How was I supposed to feel?"

"I never meant to hurt you." Jordyn gave up on trying to

stop the tears. "They told me I couldn't tell anyone. Not even my own parents. I still intended to tell you...I knew I could trust you." Her voice turned to a whisper. "But you didn't want to hear it."

She watched Chad close his eyes, as if the memories re-playing in his mind were too painful to recall.

Jordyn looked down at her boots, and blinked to keep her tears at bay. How many times had she wanted to pick up the phone and call him...tell him everything? Not being able to talk to her best friend in the world was the hardest part about the last ten years. There had never been a day that she hadn't thought of him, or a night she hadn't dreamed of him. She'd told herself he didn't care, and even convinced herself that he'd move on. But her memories and her feelings for him had never lessened, and neither had the physical pain. The man in front of her hadn't just broken her heart—he'd left it torn and mangled.

Glancing over at him, Jordyn could see she wasn't the only one who'd been hurting. But it was Christmas Eve. Instead of focusing on the negative things, she decided to change the subject. "What brought you back? I mean, to the ranch?"

He shrugged and his jaw tightened. "The same thing that brought you back, I guess. It's *home*." He stood and gathered a few small limbs from a pile before tossing them onto the fire. "I wouldn't know where else I could go. This place is helping me to heal."

Jordyn couldn't believe he was expressing his feelings so openly. It wasn't like Chad. "I know what you mean," she said, glad to have found a subject they could both agree upon.

"It's the horses. Open air. Sky that goes on forever. Maybe we should bottle it, so that others can heal too." Jordyn attempted to lighten the mood with her joke, but his face only grew more serious.

"Do you think your mother would be open to that?" He stood by the fire, his large frame appearing like a massive silhouette.

Jordyn glanced up at him. "What? Bottling up the qualities of the ranch?"

"No." He looked down as if losing his nerve. "Not exactly. But sharing it more...with people who need to heal."

Jordyn understood what he meant now and could sense the emotion in his appeal. The look on his face was one of brokenness and survival...and utter unwavering determination.

"I mean maybe during one of the slow months, just open it up to veterans. Like you said, the horses, open air, sky that goes on forever...It could help a lot of people who are hurting."

Jordyn nodded. "I think Mom would love the idea." She paused and looked up at him. "That is if you're staying and will help manage it."

He glanced over his shoulder at her. "Like I said, I don't have anywhere else to go."

Both of them remained silent a moment, staring at the mesmerizing flames of the fire. How many times had they done this together? No talking. Just comfortable being in each other's company. One of their favorite past times had been going for a ride, then lying on a blanket and staring at the endless expanse of nighttime sky that seemed to shimmer and shine. It was like gazing upon eternity.

Jordyn glanced over at him as he sat down beside her again. She found his nearness comforting and his calm demeaner reassuring. He was as familiar as moonlight to her and as beloved as the stars.

"It's really strange, isn't it?" he said.

"What is?"

"That we both ended up in that hellhole called *Terra Gardez*." He spoke as if to the night, but then turned his head and gazed down at her. "When did you find out I was there?"

Jordyn saw an unspoken pain alive and burning in his eyes, and knew hers probably reflected a similar agony. "Months later. It took me a while to recover, but I wanted to know what happened. I saw your name mentioned in the after-action report, that's all." She clenched her jaw to kill the sob, trying to keep her composure as memories assaulted her. "I didn't remember any of it for a long time, but bits and pieces come back to me every now and then."

They both left it at that. Neither one of them wanted to talk about that day that had led to the loss of one of their own. Each of them had to deal with the demons that still raised their heads when least expected.

"So you knew what I was doing all along, even though I didn't have any idea about you." He said the words thoughtfully, not in a condemning way.

"No one knew what I was doing," Jordyn replied as she thought about all the years she'd spent gathering and analyzing intelligence in foreign countries.

"I assumed you were still in the service. I didn't know you were back in the states until I saw you...here." She took a deep breath and let it out slowly, partly to control her regret and partly to hide her pain. "What was I supposed to do? Call you up and say, thanks for rescuing me? And by the way, sorry about your buddy."

"That wasn't your fault." He looked at her closely as if just realizing how much the memory affected her.

"Really?" She struggled to keep her voice from wavering. "Because if I had died on that chopper with everyone else, he'd still be alive, wouldn't he?"

She pushed herself off the bench and started to walk away, not liking where her thoughts were taking her.

"Wait." His voice was gentle but as unrelenting as an iron band.

Jordyn stopped but didn't turn around. She felt the snow lashing her face, propelled now by a strong north wind.

"I'm sorry I brought it up. I think we both need to put that day behind us." Chad moved to stand in front of her. He swept his hand across her cheek to remove the moisture there. "And maybe it's even time to start over...Completely."

Someone turned up the outside loudspeaker just then as Bing Crosby's deep voice filled the air with, *I'm Dreaming of a White Christmas.* Chad looked up at the sky and smiled. "He's got that right."

Both of them knew why someone had increased the volume. It was her father's favorite song, and brought with it a wave of memories that made Jordyn unsure whether she wanted to laugh or cry.

"*Just like the ones I used to know...*" As the crooner's voice sang the words, Chad reached for Jordon and gazed into her eyes. "Too bad we can't go back in time. We had some good Christmases, didn't we?"

A flood of memories and emotions surged through Jordyn's mind, making her unable to speak. Instead she stepped into his strong embrace and laid her head on his chest, listening to the familiar steady beating of his heart against her racing one as they swayed with the music. It *would* be nice to go back, even for just one day...To be that young naive teen who was so head-over-heels in love. Back in time to hear her father's hearty laughter and get to talk to him again.

But when Jordyn thought about how much things had changed since those days her heart skipped a beat. She found herself holding on even tighter. She didn't want to go back in time. She wanted to live for the moment, and she didn't want *this* moment to end.

"Tell me something, Jordyn," Chad said as the final notes of the song hung in the air.

"Sure." Jordyn had already told him all her secrets. She had no idea what else he wanted to know.

"Are you going to leave again?"

Jordyn slowly raised her head and gazed into his deep blue eyes. It only took a glance to find the answer she'd been seeking all along. Why had it taken so long to figure out that this was where she was supposed to be?

Home.

"No. I'm staying..." She paused and took a deep breath. "And I hope you are too."

For a long span of time, Chad said nothing. Then he bent down and lightly brushed his lips against hers, so gently and so tenderly, Jordyn barely knew it had happened.

"Sorry. There's something I need to go take care of." Chad released her without another word, and left her standing in the snow…alone.

Chapter 21

May you never be too grown up to search the skies on Christmas Eve.

– Anonymous

Jordyn headed toward the chapel along with the flow of guests for a short candlelight service. Sitting with her mother she gazed around at all the flickering candles, all united on this night in honoring the birth of Jesus. As the guests sang her favorite Christmas hymn, *O Holy Night,* Jordyn had to blink back tears. Everything about it was almost perfect. The only thing missing was Chad.

She glanced over her shoulder a few times to see if he'd come in the back, but there was no sign of his tall form anywhere in the church.

After the service she went back to the Lodge and went through the motions of helping to clean up, trying to pretend that her heart wasn't breaking all over again. Had she said something wrong? Why had Chad left so abruptly? Had he really kissed her? Or had she just imagined it? For a few moments tonight, her heart had soared and it felt like everything was falling into place. But now she was right back where she started.

One by one the volunteers finished up and departed, leaving just Jordyn and her mother to finish up. When the sleigh bells chimed on the opening door, Jordyn jerked her head around so fast she hurt her neck.

It wasn't Chad. It was a young couple—happy and in love—coming back to retrieve a purse that had been left.

"That's enough honey," her mother said to her after they'd gone. "We can finish the rest in the morning."

Jordyn nodded. "I'm coming. Just have to grab my coat. I'll turn out the lights."

Taking her time in the hopes that Chad would miraculously appear, Jordyn finally took one last look at the empty room and turned off the light. Another Christmas Gala had passed and hundreds of new Christmas memories had been made. She should have felt a sense of elation that she'd helped contribute to the feat, but she mostly just felt empty.

The wind and the snow assaulted her as soon as she opened the door, but she enjoyed its wintry bite. The forecasters had obviously been wrong about getting just a dusting. A few inches already lay on the ground and the storm showed no sign of easing.

As Jordyn traipsed toward the house, she tried to purge her gloomy thoughts by reminding herself how lucky she was. How many people got to experience the wonders of Christmas with so many loving people? And how many got to experience the delightful sight of snow on Christmas Eve—and then go to bed and enjoy the charming isolation of a warm cozy ranch house?

And then she thought of the birth of Baby Jesus and the joyous celebrations taking place all over the world on this sacred night. Before she knew it, her heart was soaring with a sensation of warmth and peace.

Jordyn stopped and looked around to get her bearings and was surprised at how little headway she'd made. The depth of the snow made it difficult to walk and the darkness of the night made it difficult to see.

As if on cue, she thought she heard sleigh bells drift to her from out of the inky blackness. *Can't be.* She looked at her phone. It was well past one o'clock in the morning. Everyone was snug in their cabins. Was she imagining the sound? Or was it a message from her father, coming from Heaven? Maybe it was just a ranch hand out on a late-night ride. She smiled at the thought that children lying wide-awake in bed would tell their parents in the morning that they had heard sleigh bells during the night. Maybe she and her mother should make that a new tradition.

But she soon found out that it wasn't a figment of her imagination. Two large horses appeared, causing her to take a step back to get out of their path. In the sleigh, hauling on the reins, sat Chad with a large smile on his face. "Sorry. I can't see the road anymore."

"What are you doing?" Jordyn looked up, more surprised than alarmed. "Do you know what time it is?"

"Yes. It's time for you to get in." He patted the seat. "It's Christmas."

"What are you—" Jordyn didn't even bother to finish the question. She jumped into the seat beside him, and was jerked back as the team took off at a steady trot. They seemed to be invigorated by the snow swirling and tumbling in every direction. The kaleidoscope of white made Jordyn dizzy, but it didn't seem to faze Chad in the least.

Over the snow they glided, sometimes under the tunneling branches of trees, sometimes across wide open fields. Snowflakes clung to her eye lashes and stung her cheeks, but Jordyn barely noticed.

Surrounded by the darkness and the swirling maze of white everything seemed enchanted, like she was part of a fairytale. She smiled as she thought of her father. No, it wasn't a fairytale, he would tell her. It's simply the magic of Christmas.

When Chad pulled the horses to a stop, Jordyn could see the giant Christmas tree in front of them. The shimmering lights on the tree made it glow like a living thing through the haze of snowflakes. She looked over at Chad. "Why are we stopping?"

"Because it's Christmas." He reached into the back of the sleigh. "And I have a present for you."

Jordyn frowned because she had nothing for him. "Why don't you wait until the morning?"

"It already is morning. And I want you to open it now."

He handed her a large bag that was heavy and rattled with a muted tone. When she pulled out the gift, the tones were no longer hushed. In the dim light, it took her a moment to realize what it was. "How did you—?" She choked and could speak no more.

He wiped a tear away from her cheek. "It wasn't supposed to make you cry."

"But it's so beautiful…and it's like my dad is right here with me again." She pulled the ring of sleigh bells close to her heart and closed her eyes. They were all here. Every sleigh bell that had been lovingly placed where she would find it, and then taken back by *Santa* on Christmas Eve, were right here, stitched together onto a piece of wide leather. A buckle had been added and the ends were clipped together to make a circle…A continuous circle of pure love. She could feel her father's spirit and could hear his hearty laughter as if he were nowhere and everywhere.

"I can't believe it." She shook the gift that had so much more meaning than just a collection of bells. Together they made the most joyous sound she had ever heard. "It's like a Christmas miracle."

"Your dad entrusted me with those bells the summer before you left." He cleared his throat. "And I was planning to give this to you the night you told me you were leaving."

Jordyn looked at the circle of bells more closely. "So you *made* this?" The leather was old, but supple and well-oiled. Chad had probably rescued a discarded piece of old harness and carefully brought it back to life.

"I wanted you to have them all together in one place. That's the only way I could think of to do it." He pointed to one of the bells. "But your dad did the hard part. Over the years, he engraved each one with the year you found it."

Jordyn lifted the piece and studied the bells. Along with each date was engraved a single word. *Believe. Joy. Snow. Tree.* Each word was associated with something that happened that year, and each one brought back a vivid memory that Jordyn had thought long forgotten. One word was all she needed to spark the memory.

"This is the year I helped cut down one of the Christmas trees." She held it up for Chad to see, and pointed to the word *tree*. "I think I was twelve. And this is the year that it snowed a foot on Christmas Eve." She looked up excitedly. "Do you remember?"

Chad nodded. "Yes, I remember." He pointed to the last bell on the chain. "Do you know what this one means?"

Jordyn studied the word: *Ring*. She looked up. "I'm not sure about that one. I guess it just signifies the ringing of the bells. And that I should always remember the magical tones?"

Chad pointed to the date. "Actually, this one isn't from your father."

Jordyn looked more closely at the date. "That's *this* year." She gazed up at him, confused, and then back at the bell. The engraved date and word weren't as precise and elegant as her father's had been, as if the etching had been hurriedly—or perhaps, nervously—done.

He nodded. "Your father never gave me the last one...the year you left...so I had to add one of my own. That's what took me so long."

"What does ring—"

Chad pulled a small box out of his pocket. "Oh, I almost forgot. That's what took me so long. I also had to find this."

Jordyn stared at the box and the trembling hand that held it. For all of his strength and confidence, she could see how emotional Chad was.

"Will you marry me, Jordyn?"

Jordyn answered by throwing her arms around his neck.

"Yes! Yes!"

"Then take your mitten off so I can get this on your finger before it falls into the snow," he said, laughing.

Jordyn hurriedly removed the glove and waited for Chad to open the box and place the ring on her finger. Both hands were trembling, but they blamed it on the cold, not their nerves.

"Merry Christmas, Jordyn." He held her face in his hands, his voice thick and unsteady. "I'm sorry I didn't trust and believe you. But I never stopped loving you."

"I never stopped loving you either." Although she could barely see now through the haze that filled her eyes, Jordyn pointed to the piece of leather again. "There's a space here. What's that for?"

"It's from the last year you were here." He ran his hand over the smooth leather. "I decided to leave room in case we find the missing bell someday. Your mother said she'd keep her eye out for it."

"So Mom knows about all this?" Jordyn waved her hand in the air, admiring the sparkling ring.

"No. She only knows I was looking for the lost sleigh bell." He leaned down and kissed her gently, slowly, and affectionately, yet with a longing intimacy. "I wanted you to be the one to tell your mother."

Jordyn felt like her heart was going to burst—or melt. His touch was almost unbearable in its tenderness and the look on his face so galvanizing, it sent a tremor through her. When he laced his fingers with hers, a new surge of affection brought a mist of joy to her eyes.

Even though the snow whipped and swirled around them, Jordyn had never felt so warm and comfortable. This was a Christmas she would never forget.

And she didn't want it to end.

Chapter 22

Christmas is the day that holds all time together.
— Alexander Smith

Christmas Day

Jordyn knew her mother would probably sleep in a little on Christmas day. Who could blame her? As hard as she'd been working, she'd finally put another year of festivities behind her. But Jordyn could hardly contain herself as she waited in the living room and watched the clock.

To help pass the time, she stood in front of the towering family Christmas tree, staring at its overflowing branches, and touching one or two of the ornaments lightly. Just a jumble of decorations to most people, but each one held a special memory for Jordyn. A handmade ball covered with glitter from a six-year-old Jordyn here. An intricately designed Christmas bell from her teenage years there.

Some of the pieces sparked instant memories. Others were stored more deeply, and rose to the surface only after careful consideration.

When her mother at last walked into the living room and saw Chad pacing in front of the fireplace, she stopped in her tracks.

"Merry Christmas, Mrs. Dunaway," he said politely, as if his presence wasn't anything out of the ordinary.

"Merry Christmas, Chad." She recovered and walked over to give him a kiss on the cheek. "What are you—"

"I wanted him here when I showed you what he gave me." Jordyn pulled the sleigh bells out of the bag and gave them a shake. "Look. Can you believe it?"

"The sleigh bells." Mrs. Dunaway looked over at Chad with watery eyes. "It's beautiful! Now I know why you were asking for the missing one."

When she glanced back at Jordyn, she threw her hand over her mouth in surprise. "What's *that*?" She pointed to the ring on Jordyn's finger.

"Oh, just another gift Chad has been waiting to give me. Isn't it beautiful?"

When her mother didn't say anything, Jordyn reached out with a steadying hand. Her Mom looked so pale, Jordyn thought for a moment she was going to faint. "Are you okay?"

"Yes, I'm fine." Mrs. Dunaway shuffled over to the tree, and picked up a small package. "It startled me for a minute, that's all. But I shouldn't be surprised."

"Is this for me?" Jordyn took the box and sat down cross-legged on the floor near the tree.

"I guess it's actually for both of you," Mrs. Dunaway said, her voice still full of bewilderment.

As Jordyn stripped away the ribbon, Mrs. Dunaway continued to talk. "When Chad asked me to look for the missing bell, I remembered that Shawn had engraved one for you… but I never saw it. I had no idea what he'd done with it."

Jordyn lifted the lid of the box and pulled away the bright red tissue paper inside.

"I found that yesterday in the bottom of the closet when I was searching for a bolo tie for Chad to wear to the Gala." She swiped a quick tear from her eye. "I mean I've been in that closet hundreds of times, but I never noticed it before." Her eyes sought and lingered on a large picture of her husband on the wall beside the tree. "It was right there, lying on the floor in the back. Directly beside the box of bolos."

Jordyn gasped when she saw the sleigh bell and Chad's eyes grew large. "It's the missing bell, isn't it?"

"Yes, it's the missing bell. Merry Christmas—from your mother *and* your father."

A single tear trickled out of Jordyn's eye as she saw the engraved date. It was the year she'd left Painted Sky ranch to begin her new career. She glanced up and smiled, knowing her father was looking down from Heaven. He had a hand in this miraculous find—and everyone knew it. The essence of him filled this room. The only thing missing was his booming laugh and joyful smile.

Jordyn handed the bell to Chad so he could take a closer look. When he saw the single word her father had engraved all those years before, she watched his blue eyes turn misty. "How—" He stopped, unable to continue.

Jordyn wondered the same thing. The gift was the perfect conclusion to their perfect love story...a love story that had not been denied or delayed—but merely, destined.

Because how could her father have known then that the sleigh bell would remain hidden until now? And how could he have guessed that it would be found on the same day that his daughter became engaged?

What is it luck? Coincidence?

Or another Christmas miracle?

Because the word inscribed on the magical sleigh bell was: *Love.*

Do you BELIEVE?

I hope you enjoyed reading SLEIGH BELLS RING!

Christmas is a time of wonder, traditions, and special magical moments that I hope I captured in this novel. I had a wonderful time reminiscing about my own childhood, which sparked memories of chestnuts roasting on an open fire and the sounds of Christmas music filling the air.

If you're like me and believe in twists of fate, true love, and the magic of Christmas, then you will love a family-owned business I discovered while writing this novel. Called Magical Bells, the company fashions its sleigh bells after the iconic *'First Gift of Christmas'* featured in the movie *Polar Express*. They are faithful in every detail, resulting in beautiful, handcrafted, heirloom-quality bells.

Gift-giving is only one facet of Christmas, and there are many ways to celebrate the holiday season that don't involve buying presents. A special family tradition can be as simple as making popcorn garland to hang on the tree, enjoying a mug of hot chocolate on Christmas Eve, or baking and decorating cookies.

Of course, the best Christmas tradition of all is spending time with the ones we love, while remembering the true reason for the season.

I hope you and yours have a holiday full of magical moments that will be remembered for years to come!

Jessica James

OTHER BOOKS BY JESSICA JAMES

Award-Winning Women's Fiction

LACEWOOD

Award-Winning Romantic Suspense

PRESIDENTIAL ADVANTAGE

DEADLINE (Phantom Force Tactical Book 1)

FINE LINE (Phantom Force Tactical Book 2)

FRONT LINE (Phantom Force Tactical Book 3)

PHANTOM FORCE TACTICAL SERIES SET Books 1-3

PROTECTING ASHLEY

MEANT TO BE: A Novel of Honor and Duty

Award-Winning Historical Fiction

THE LION OF THE SOUTH

SHADES OF GRAY: UNABRIDGED (LOST CHAPTERS)

SHADES OF GRAY: A Novel of the Civil War in Virginia

NOBLE CAUSE (Book 1 Heroes Through History)

ABOVE & BEYOND (Book 2 Heroes Through History)

LIBERTY & DESTINY (Book 3 Heroes Through History)

HEROES THROUGH HISTORY BOXED SET (Books 1-3)

BONUS MATERIAL

FINE LINE

(Phantom Force Tactical Book 2)

Blake Madison reached for the alarm at the first ding so it wouldn't wake his wife.

"It's Saturday," Cait said sleepily, reaching for his arm. "Sleep in."

"I'm going for a quick run." He crawled out from under the covers, carefully moving their dog's head off his legs. "It's a lot of pressure having a young trophy wife. I have to stay in shape."

She threw a pillow at him, but then reached over and ran her hand over his abs. "You're doing a pretty good job of staying in shape."

The comment made Blake smile. He had gotten back into a weightlifting and running routine shortly after getting married, and was in almost as good a shape now as he had been when he was a young Navy SEAL. Then again, Cait was pretty fit herself. She had taken over most of the barn chores, and actually enjoyed splitting and stacking wood. She was always

amused when other women saw her toned arms and request-
ed the contact information for her personal trainer.

Dressing as quietly as he could in a pair of sweatpants and
tee shirt, Blake headed toward the door.

"You forgot something," he heard from beneath the covers.

He went back and bent over her. "I know. But I was afraid
I'd be tempted to crawl back into bed."

"Good answer." She reached up, grabbed a handful of his
shirt, and pulled him down for a kiss, causing him to linger.

Sitting on the side of the bed, he leaned down with his
hands propped on each side of her pillow. "Do you know
how much I love you, Mrs. Madison?"

She grinned sleepily and pulled him close again. "Show
me."

"I just did that a few hours ago. Remember?"

"Umm hmm." She drew the words out with her eyes still
closed and a contented smile on her face. "But that was last
night."

He glanced at the door, then back at the bed.

She must have sensed his hesitation. "I'm just kidding. We
have all day. Go for your run."

Blake lifted her hand off the covers and kissed it. "We've
been married almost a year. We need to start acting like an old
married couple, not newlyweds."

"Are you saying you want me to become a nag?"

"Only if you nag me about getting back into bed with you."

He gave her another long kiss, and then stood and stared
down at her in the dim light. She was wearing his NAVY tee

shirt—or as she called it, her favorite negligée—with one arm lying on top of the blankets. His gaze fell on her wedding band, and then drifted to her tousled hair spread out on the pillow and her long lashes resting on her cheeks. He reconsidered his need for outdoor exercise.

"Bring me a cup of coffee when you get back," she murmured, pulling the covers up and rolling over.

"I won't be long, baby." He headed toward the door and patted his leg for the dog to follow. "I'll take Max so you don't have to get up and let him out."

"Love you."

His heart flipped. "Love you more."

Just as he started to close the door, she spoke again. *"Don't miss me too much."*

He grinned as the door clicked shut. She always said that when he left, even if they were only going to be separated for a few minutes. It had become a routine. Even the kids said it now when they left for school or went to visit a friend.

Heading down the stairs he turned off the security alarm and went out onto the porch, taking a deep breath of the cool morning air. After doing a couple of stretches, he sprinted down the lane with Max trotting along beside, his heart bursting with happiness and contentment.

These early morning runs were as much for his mental wellbeing as for physical training. He usually used the time to clear his mind and focus on his business goals for the day. But as he listened to the cadence of his feet hitting the dirt road and the sound of his steady breathing, his mind drifted to his upcoming anniversary instead.

He wanted to come up with something really special to celebrate—something that would show Cait how much she meant to him and the kids. It had been on his mind for weeks, but now the milestone moment loomed just days away and he still didn't know what that *something* was.

Moving to the side of the lane to avoid a large mud puddle, his mind continued to drift and wander. He thought back to the day he'd proposed, causing the vivid memories to replay through his mind like a movie.

Cait had just finished testifying at a congressional hearing, and was waiting for him by the Washington Monument. He'd snuck up behind her and grabbed her around the waist with one hand and the shoulders with the other. Drawing her up against him, he'd whispered in her ear. "Come here often?"

She'd tried to turn around and look up at him, but he held her firmly with her back pressed against him. "If that's your best pick-up line, you're going to be a lonely man," she'd said.

"Really? It works in the movies."

"Sorry. But, no."

"Okay. How about this?" He'd leaned down and whispered in her ear. "Hey, baby. Wanna ride in my truck?"

"Now you sound downright creepy," she'd said. "That's a definite no."

"Okay. Let me see… Close your eyes this time."

"All right. They're closed."

"Hey, sweetheart." He had let go of her then and backed away. "Are you free?"

"I don't know." She'd laughed, but continued to stand with her back to him. "When?"

"The rest of your life."

Whether it had been his words or the seriousness of his tone he didn't know, but she'd turned around with a perplexed expression on her face—and found him down on one knee. His children Drew and Whitney held a sign that said, *Will you marry us?*

Blake smiled at the memory. Her surprise and the children's pure delight at being a part of the occasion had forged a memory he would never forget as long as he lived.

Bypassing the security gate and turning left at the end of their long driveway Blake continued toward the main road, his breath coming faster now and creating short bursts of steam in the chilly morning air.

The gate made his thoughts wander back still further, to when he and Cait had testified against Senator Wiley and his ex-wife, Mallory. They'd tried to keep a low profile and return to their private lives, but the media attention and social media campaigns from political fanatics made that impossible.

There had been lots of intimidating communication and a few death threats immediately following the scandal, so despite the home's isolation, Blake had taken the extra steps of installing an electronic gate to stop vehicles, and upgraded the security system in the house.

The addition of Max and the fact that his house was a sort of informal headquarters for his security firm, made him feel pretty secure and confident that his family was protected. There was rarely a day when at least one former Navy SEAL did not stop by or spend the night—and depending on deployments for his company, there were often half a dozen or more.

Blake inhaled the musty smell of dying leaves and contemplated the gold and red colors splashed like a painter's canvas all around him. It was Cait's favorite time of year, and was beginning to be his as well. They'd harvested the last of the vegetables and pumpkins from the garden, and spent any free time together stacking wood in preparation for the coming winter. Somehow it wasn't work when Cait was involved. It was pure pleasure.

Passing the two-and-a-half-mile mark he knew by heart, Blake slowed down. The image of Cait lying in bed turned him around before he'd made it to the main road. If the kids were still asleep, maybe he'd take a quick shower and re-join her.

Sprinting the last hundred yards, Blake was surprised when Max didn't follow him up the porch, but continued around the side of the house with his nose to the ground. The dog usually had a pretty hearty appetite after a run and wanted fed immediately.

"Where you going, boy? Smell a raccoon or something?"

Blake let him go and entered the house to find his young daugher Whitney walking slowly down the stairs. She appeared disheveled, but looked wide awake. *So much for going back to bed.* "What are you doing up so early, young lady?"

He didn't hear her answer as he continued into the kitchen to turn on the coffee, and splash his face with water. With the coffee starting to brew, he stood in the glow of the open refrigerator door, trying to figure out what he could whip up. Maybe he'd surprise Cait with breakfast in bed as an early anniversary gift.

Whitney shuffled into the room behind him and noisily pulled out a chair at the small kitchen table. "When is Cait coming back?"

"What, honey?" Blake continued staring into the fridge. Having just turned four, Whitney talked a lot, but didn't always make sense.

"When are those men going to bring her back?"

Blake closed the refrigerator door slowly as a twinge of dread crawled up his spine. He turned to Whitney and knelt down beside her. "What men, honey? What are you talking about?"

"The mean ones that came." Her eyes brimmed with tears.

Blake didn't ask any more questions. He stood and turned in one movement.

Racing to the stairs, he took them two at a time and headed at a full sprint down the hallway to the master bedroom. He tried to open the door quietly, hoping to find Cait still sleeping, but he almost tore the door off its hinges in his urgency.

The bed was empty.

Order FINE LINE (Book 2) today!
All books in this series can stand alone.
Available wherever books are sold!

Visit www.jessicajamesbooks.com

Find Out What Everyone's Talking About!

Lacewood

2020 John Esten Cooke Award for Fiction
Finalist in Greater Detroit RWA Booksellers Best contest
Finalist in HOLT Medallion contest

History, mystery, and a love story that spans centuries…

A disillusioned socialite and a wounded special operations veteran find a way to save an abandoned house from neglect. A haunting read that vividly conveys the heartache of war, the tragedy of loss, and the fulfillment of destiny…even when souls are separated by centuries. Part love story, part ghost story, Lacewood is a timeless novel about trusting in fate, letting go of the past, and believing in things that can't be seen.

MOVING TO A SMALL TOWN in Virginia is a big change for New York socialite Katie McCain. But when she stumbles across an abandoned 200-year-old mansion, she's enthralled by the enduring beauty of the neglected estate—and captivated by the haunting portrait of a woman in mourning.

Purchasing the property on a whim, Katie attempts to fit in with the colorful characters in the town of New Hope, while trying to unravel the mystery of the "widow of Lacewood." As she pieces together the previous owner's heartrending story, Katie uncovers secrets the house has held for centuries, and discovers the key to coming to terms with her own sense of loss.

The past and present converge when hometown hero Will Durham returns and begins his own healing process by helping the "city girl" restore the place that holds so many memories. As the mystic web of destiny is woven, a love story that might have been lost forever is exposed, and a destiny that has been waiting in the shadows for centuries is fulfilled.

Shades of Gray

Honor and conviction clash with loyalty and love in this epic Civil War love story that pits brother against brother. **Shades of Gray** chronicles the clash of a Confederate cavalry officer with a Union spy as they defend their beliefs, their country, and their honor.

What readers say about Shades of Gray…

"If you want to read a book you will never forget and will think about for months after reading it, read Shades of Gray. It took my breath away. Honestly, you will not sleep."

"My house is a mess, my sink is piled high with dishes and my husband ate watermelon for dinner because I could not put down Shades of Gray. Could. Not. Put. Down. Honestly, this book completely captivated me and left me emotionally drained. I loved it!!!"

"I've not been much of a reader and was given Shades of Gray. I've read it five times and fall in love every time I read it. Because of you I have developed a love for reading."

"It is now 1 a.m. cause I couldn't put down my I-pad with your delicious novel. Thank you for the pleasure you afforded this 81 year old."

"Wonderful, fabulous book! I seldom reflect back on a book, but this one has haunted me since I finished it at 2 a.m."

"Could hardly work or sleep until I read the last page."

"Lost a lot of sleeping reading this one. Too good to put down! Made me laugh. Made me cry. Awesome book!"

"I loved this novel. Still crying, but I laughed just as much as I cried."

"Bravo! One of the best books I have read on the Civil War. Absolutely could not put it down. Please do not stop writing."

"I can't remember having such a heavy heart and crying so much since reading Gone with the Wind. Thank you!"

"Loved. Loved. Needs to be made into a movie."

Shades of Gray *(Continued)*

"I'm not usually one for Civil War era books, but I've got to say you really got me on this one. I LOVE it!"

"Oh my, I let the world go on around me and could hardly put it down. Every free moment, every break at work. LOVED IT!!!"

"I was completely lost and spellbound by the realistic story. Without hesitation I must say this now ranks equally with Gone With The Wind."

"Though a male I liked it, and recommended it to my wife."

"I stayed up until 2 a.m. two nights in a row because I couldn't put it down. It was a book that I couldn't wait to read, yet I didn't want it to end!"

"This book has touched me more than any other I have ever read. I cried, laughed, and then cried some more. Thank you for such an amazing and touching story."

"If someone said I could only ever have one book for the rest of my life either of these [Shades of Gray or Noble Cause] would be my pick. Thank you."

"I know a book is very good when I think about it after I complete the book, and I cannot start another one right away. Five star rating for sure."

"This book absolutely ripped my heart out. Superb. Thank you for such a moving, believable love story."

"I have not read a romance novel in probably 10 years. Your book was so good for my soul."

Don't miss reading this novel! Available wherever books are sold.

About the Author

Jessica James is an award-winning author of fiction and non-fiction ranging from the Revolutionary War to modern day. She is a four-time winner of the John Esten Cooke Award for Southern Fiction and numerous other literary awards.

James' novels appeal to both men and women, and are featured in library collections all over the United States including Harvard and the U.S. Naval Academy.

Connect with her at jessicajamesbooks.com.

Join her newsletter and receive free content:
www.subscribepage.com/jessicajamesnews

Email Jessica@JessicaJamesBooks.com

BookBub: Bookbub.com/authors/jessica-james
Facebook: Facebook.com/romantichistoricalfiction
Pinterest: pinterest.com/southernromance
GoodReads: goodreads.com/jessicajames